Cat's pulse was hammering. How could she tell him the rest now, with her body aching for something she didn't really understand?

"About—about the husband you'll find me. The one who'll agree to a divorce."

Jake swung around and faced her. "Cat, I just told you. A man with enough money to agree not to touch yours won't see any reason to go into a temporary marriage."

"Am I pretty, Jake?"

"You know you are," he said in a voice rough as gravel.

"And—and I'm untouched. I'm a virgin."

Did she think he didn't know that? It was all that had kept him from taking her a minute ago, from stripping her naked, cupping her hips.

"What's your point?"

"My point," she said slowly, "is that the man I marry will be my legal husband. For a day, a week, a month—I'll be his wife. And…"

"And?"

"And I'll give him the only gift he can't buy." She swallowed. "I'll give him my virginity— and you're going to teach me how to do it."

Sandra Marton

THE DISOBEDIENT VIRGIN

The Ramirez' Brides

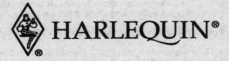

HARLEQUIN®

TORONTO • NEW YORK • LONDON
AMSTERDAM • PARIS • SYDNEY • HAMBURG
STOCKHOLM • ATHENS • TOKYO • MILAN • MADRID
PRAGUE • WARSAW • BUDAPEST • AUCKLAND

ISBN 0-373-12499-6

THE DISOBEDIENT VIRGIN

First North American Publication 2005.

This edition published by arrangement with Harlequin Books S.A.

® and TM are trademarks of the publisher. Trademarks indicated with ® are registered in the United States Patent and Trademark Office, the Canadian Trade Marks Office and in other countries.

www.eHarlequin.com

Printed in U.S.A.

CHAPTER ONE

THE day Jake Ramirez's life turned upside down began like any other.

He rose at six, had his first cup of strong black coffee while he scanned the *New York Times,* drank his second after he'd shaved and showered. A few minutes after seven, dressed in a dark gray suit, white shirt and navy tie, he took the private elevator from his Fifth Avenue duplex to the marble lobby.

His black Mercedes waited at the curb. The driver had been with him a long time and knew better than to leap from the car to open and close the door for his boss. Jake had homes on both coasts and was rumored to own half the skyscrapers in Manhattan, but old habits died hard.

People who worked for Jake Ramirez were not his servants.

"Morning, Mr. Ramirez."

"Good morning, Dario."

His driver pulled into traffic. As always, Jake spent a couple of minutes engaging him in small talk. Would the Jets win Sunday's game? Had his eldest daughter won the part she'd tried out for in the school play? Then, also as always, Dario raised the privacy partition, Jake took out his cell phone and started his day.

First, a call to his office. He had a breakfast meeting at the Stock Exchange but he wanted to touch base with his P.A. Belle was almost as much a workaholic as he was; she might already be at her desk.

Not today, though. Jake left a message on her answering machine as the car headed downtown. It saved time, and time was a precious commodity when you headed something the size of Ramirez Enterprises.

Calls to people he was currently doing business with came next. Jake took no notes—he had a prodigious memory—as he reassured one, questioned another, told a third he'd fly out at the end of the week to deal personally with a developing problem.

The cell phone rang before he could dial again. Jake checked the incoming number as he brought the phone to his ear.

"Good morning, Belle."

"Good morning, Mr. Ramirez. I thought I'd better remind you that it's Miss Vickers's birthday."

Jake closed his eyes. Hell. He'd forgotten all about it, despite the hints Samantha had been dropping—hints about diamond solitaires, though he'd made it clear enough that wasn't on the agenda.

"Right. Well, phone the—"

"Florist. I already did. Two dozen roses. Red."

"Fine, fine. And phone—"

"Tiffany's. They'll deliver a sapphire bracelet at noon."

"Sapphire?"

"Miss Vickers has blue eyes," Belle said, so crisply that he could almost hear the unspoken reprimand within the simple words. Wouldn't it be nice if he paid attention to such things? He never did, though. After a while, beautiful women were all the same. "I made you an eight-thirty dinner reservation at Sebastian's. A booth in the front room, of course."

"Of course," Jake said, smiling. "And you did all that this morning?" He flashed a look at his watch. "I didn't think anybody was open at this hour."

"They're all open for you," Belle said dryly. "Just in case you don't want Sebastian's, I made back-up reservations at Leonie's. Tell me which you prefer and I'll cancel the other.''

''What's Sebastian's?''

''It's new. No mention of it yet in the papers. It's in the meat-packing district. The buzz is that Madonna was spotted there last week,'' Belle paused. ''Miss Vickers will like it.''

Jake grinned. Was there a hint of distaste in his P.A.'s tone? He suspected she didn't approve of Samantha Vickers. His mother didn't, either, even though—maybe especially since—she'd only seen Sam on the T.V., sashaying down the runway in the Emmeline's Lingerie primetime special, wearing little more than a garter belt, a thong, a wisp of lace, a pair of stiletto heels and a look that said she couldn't be tamed unless you had a very, very large…whip.

''Your name has been linked with hers in the paper but you've never brought her here,'' Sarah Reece had told him. ''I figured this was my chance to get a look at her.''

He never brought any of the women he dated to his mother's condo, Jake had thought, but he'd wisely kept silent.

''That outfit Miss Vickers was wearing…'' Pink had swept into his mother's cheeks. Jake had done all he could not to roll his eyes. Sometimes, he thought Sarah was a throwback to an earlier time. She was so prim. So proper. He loved her for it, but he really wasn't in the mood for where he knew the conversation was heading. ''Joaquim, it's time you settled down. All these young women you date… I know the world has changed, but—''

''But, you'd like me to find a nice, old-fashioned girl.''

''Yes.''

''Marry her.''

''Oh, yes.''

''Have a houseful of kids, a dog, trade the Porsche and the Mercedes for a station wagon and a van—''

''Now you're making fun of me,'' his mother said, and

Jake had put his arms around her, assured her that he wasn't, that he'd do all those things some day.

But not yet.

Not yet, when the city, when the world, was brimming with Samanthas. More to the point, not when building his empire was still the most important thing in Jake's life.

"If you don't like Sebastian's or Leonie's," Belle said, dragging his thoughts into the present, "I can call that French place on—"

"Sebastian's is fine. What would I do without you, Bellissima?"

"Cross your wires again, probably, and get your face on Page Six by sending roses to a woman you stopped seeing a month before."

"Once," Jake said. "I only did that once."

"Once was enough," Belle said, with the crisp assurance of a woman who'd been with her boss since he'd made his first million. "All right, then. After your breakfast appointment, you have a meeting with—"

"I know."

"And late lunch at Gracie Mansion with the Mayor."

"Belle," Jake said with a touch of amused impatience, "have I ever forgotten a business appointment? Now, is there anything new?"

"No. Wait… Kelsey just brought me something from the reception desk."

"What is it?"

"A large padded envelope. She says it was hand-delivered."

"Well, open it."

"I already did. There's a letter inside, sealed, and—"

"And it smells of perfume." Jake sighed. Some women were persistent, even though he always made his intentions, or lack of them, clear. "Just toss it."

"No perfume. In fact, it's quite formal-looking. Heavy

vellum, no return address…but it says *'confidencial'* as well as 'private.'''

Jake frowned. Belle wasn't a *latina* but she'd pronounced the word *con-fee-den-see-al* so clearly that he could almost see the non-English spelling.

''Spanish?''

''I suppose. The postmark says 'Brasil'.''

''Then it's Portuguese,'' Jake said, his frown deepening. Who'd be sending him a confidential letter from Brazil? He'd done some business in Argentina, but he'd never even been to Brazil.

''And there's something else,'' Belle said. ''A box. A small white one, the kind you'd get at a jeweler's. Shall I open both the letter and the box, Mr. Ramirez?''

Belle had been with him a very long time, and he had few secrets from her, but a gut feeling was suddenly telling him to be cautious. He'd had made his fortune following his instincts. Why deny them now?

''No, that's all right. Just put both of them on my desk. I'll deal with them later.''

And undoubtedly discover that the letter was a clever advertisement for a time share in Rio and that the box held a small gift to encourage his interest, Jake thought cynically as he ended the call.

Sometimes, having money was a pain in the ass.

His day went well.

The president of the Stock Exchange was amenable to Jake taking a seat on the board, the Mayor liked his idea for a spring fund-raising event for the city's ever-expanding homeless population, and the head of the Arab conglomerate that owned a building on Park Avenue Jake wanted to buy had finally decided the price he'd offered was acceptable.

Samantha phoned him twice, first to thank him for the

flowers, and then for the bracelet and to tell him they'd been invited to a house party in Connecticut the next weekend.

"I'll have to check my calendar and see if I'm free," he told her, even though he already knew that he was. He wasn't a big fan of house parties. Too many people wanting things from him—the men sidling up to him with false smiles, the women groping him under the table at dinner. But Sam enjoyed them and, at just three weeks into their affair, pleasing her was less a burden than he knew it would eventually become.

Jake was nothing if not a realist. His childhood on the mean streets of the South Bronx had ensured that.

Dario dropped him at his office a few minutes before seven in the evening. He was running late but he always made a point of stopping there at the end of the day if he was in town. It was an old habit, a need to make sure nothing had turned up that needed his personal or immediate attention.

Everyone was gone, even Belle. Jake's footsteps echoed against the marble floor as he made his way past the reception area, down a couple of corridors to his own private domain. He switched on the lights, illuminating a room three times the size of the apartment where he'd grown up, and crossed the Aubusson carpet to his desk.

He scanned the page of notes Belle had left him, scribbled a couple of comments in the margins, then reached for the phone to call Sam and tell her he'd be a little late. His gaze fell on the vellum envelope and the small white box that lay next to it. In all the events of the day, he'd forgotten about them.

He picked up the box. What would it contain? he wondered with amusement. He'd received unsolicited gifts from upscale marketers before, everything from leather-bound appointment books to sterling silver key rings. This was most likely a key ring; the box was too small to hold a book.

Jake put it down and reached for the envelope. There were the words 'private' and '*confidencial*,' just as Belle had described, along with the Brazilian postmark. He raised the envelope to his nose. Belle had been right about that, too. No smell whatsoever, except, he thought wryly, for a whiff of self-importance.

As offers for time shares went, this one was definitely aimed at the top.

He slit the envelope with a letter-opener and unfolded the single sheet of paper inside. The letterhead read "Javier Estes & Associados, OAB, Rio de Janeiro," but the letter itself was in English.

Dear Mr. Ramirez
My name is Javier Estes. I am the senior partner at the legal firm of Javier Estes & Associates…

A couple of lines later, Jake sank into his chair. The enormous room seemed suddenly small and airless.

Everything he'd grown up believing was false.

The father he'd grown up venerating had not existed.

He was not the son of a poor Hispanic boy who'd died a hero in a vicious, unheralded war in the jungles of South America. According to the letter in Jake's hand, he was the son of a wealthy Brazilian who'd died in bed just a few months ago.

The attorney's words spelled out a brutal story. Thirty-one years before, during a trip to New York, Enrique Ramirez had engaged in a brief affair with Sarah Reece. He'd gotten her pregnant, gone back to Brazil and never contacted her again.

Jake was the fruit of that union.

There was more, things even more impossible than that heart-stopping revelation, but Jake wouldn't bother with them now. He couldn't; it was too much. Instead, he reread the part of the letter that made a lie of everything he believed in, everything his mother had told him.

His gaze dropped to the last paragraph.

In the final months of his life, my client regretted the errors of his youth and sought to make amends to those he had wronged. In accordance with his wishes, I enclose a small token of his concern for your mother. Please give it to her on Senhor Ramirez's behalf.

Jake scooped up the unopened box, almost crushed it in his fist. Twenty minutes later, jaw set, mouth a grim line, he marched through the lobby of his mother's apartment building on Sutton Place. The doorman began to greet him but Jake didn't break stride as he headed for the elevator.

"Don't announce me," he said.

He had a key to his mother's apartment but he didn't use it. Instead, he stabbed the bell hard enough to damn near shove it through the jamb. He saw the peephole slide aside and then the door swung open.

"Joaquim," his mother said happily. Her smile faded. "Joaquim? What's happened?"

"I don't know, Mother," Jake said coldly. "You tell me."

He stepped into the foyer, elbowed the door closed and thrust the envelope at her. He watched her look at it, heard her soft intake of breath as she read the postmark. Her eyes flashed to his.

"Read it," he snapped.

Sarah nodded. Her hands, her entire body, trembled. Who would write to her son from Brazil? Who would write something that would make her son so furious?

Who? she thought, as her long-buried secret rose like a wraith from the distant past and revealed itself in black ink on creamy vellum.

Sarah read the letter. She looked up, searching desperately for the right words, the ones that would ease the anger, the pain in her boy's eyes.

"Joaquim. It was all a long time ago…"

Jake thrust a small white box at her. "He sent this for you."

Sarah stared at the box. "I don't—I can't imagine—Joaquim, please, you must listen—"

"Open it!"

She did. An emerald ring winked up at her, its heart as cold as her own. A card was tucked alongside.

For Sarah, it read. *My beautiful dove.*

Sarah Reece looked up at her son. And fainted.

She was on the sofa when she came to, a cold cloth on her brow. Joaquim squatted beside her.

"Are you all right?" he said. His tone was still chilly but there was, at least, concern in his eyes.

She nodded. "I'm fine." He held out a hand as she started to sit up and she took it, not because she needed the support but because she was afraid of losing her son.

A muscle bunched in his jaw. "It's true, then."

She swallowed dryly. "Yes."

"My father wasn't a soldier."

"No."

"He didn't die a hero's death."

"No," Sarah said, her voice soft and shaky.

"And," Jake said, his mouth twisting, "it sure as hell wasn't a sweet, romantic love story interrupted by war."

"I was young. Painfully young. I'd been raised in a very strict home and—and I knew little about the world. I know this is difficult for you but you have to understand, Joaquim—"

"Do not call me that," Jake snapped. "My name is Jake."

"Joaquim—"

"It's Jake, damn it! I'm American, not Brazilian."

"Jake." The name tasted foreign on Sarah's tongue. "Son, please try and understand. I met your father—"

"Call him Enrique. Or Ramirez. But whatever you do don't refer to him ever again as my father."

"I was working in a shop. He came in to buy something. He was handsome and charming, and I—"

"You slept with him," Jake said coldly, "and he left you when he learned you were carrying his bastard."

"No!" Sarah rose to her feet. "He never knew."

"Why? Why didn't you tell him?"

Jake's eyes held a glimmer of hope. Sarah knew what he wanted to hear, something romantic about her not wanting to burden Enrique with the truth, but she'd lied enough. She'd buried herself in lies years ago.

"I couldn't," she said quietly. "By the time I realized I was carrying a child, your—Enrique was gone."

"And you had no way to reach him," Jake said bitterly.

"None." This was the final humiliation. "The only thing I had to remember him by was you, Joaq—you, Jake. And I loved you, always, with all my heart."

"You lied to me," he said tonelessly. "My whole damned life has been a lie. All that crap about honoring the memory of my old man, the hero—"

"Would you rather I'd told you the truth?"

She had a point, but Jake wasn't in the mood to concede it.

"You didn't have to embroider it the way you did."

"At first, it was enough to let you think your father was dead, but things changed. You were seventeen, you were running with a bad crowd—and then you got into serious trouble." Her voice took on a touch of anger. "I did what I had to, to keep you from prison."

Jake stared at his mother. She looked as if she'd aged a decade in the last few minutes.

"I did what I thought best," she said.

In his heart, he knew that. Right or wrong, what she'd done was for him. By the time he was seventeen, he hadn't given a damn about anything. He hated school, hated the slum they lived in, hated the bleak future that swallowed everyone he knew.

He'd "borrowed" a Cadillac, taken it joy-riding. To impress his friends? To impress himself? To this day, he didn't know the answer. All he knew was that after he was caught, his mother had worked miracles.

First she'd talked a stern-faced judge out of sending him to a juvenile facility with a story that would have softened any heart. She'd spoken of a young couple in love, of a soldier who was only a boy, of his death on foreign soil and the child he had not lived to see.

Then she'd convinced Jake to use his intelligence to get good grades and a university scholarship instead of using it to get into even worse trouble.

"*If you won't do it for yourself, Joaquim,*" she'd said, "*do it to honor the memory of your father.*"

And he had.

Jake turned toward his mother and looked at her again. He saw her as she must have been when she met Enrique Ramirez. Young, probably innocent, swept off her feet by a rich man with too much money and no morals, if the rest of the letter was true.

He'd almost forgotten the rest of the letter.

"Jake?"

Jake squeezed his mother's hand. For now, that was as close as he could come to acceptance.

"I baked this morning," Sarah said, a hesitant smile curving her lips. "That apple cake you like so much... Unless you're busy this evening."

Busy? He was supposed to be at Samantha's in half an hour but she, the glitter of New York, the life he'd made for himself, seemed light-years away.

"No," he said, "I'm not busy." He cleared his throat. "I'm never too busy for your apple cake, Mama."

He held a smile until Sarah left the room. Then he picked up the letter and sank down on the sofa, smoothing out the heavy paper with his hand.

The second paragraph was almost as shocking as the first.

According to Enrique Ramirez's last will and testament, his fling with Sarah Reece hadn't been the only dalliance that had resulted in a pregnancy.

Ramirez had sired two other illegitimate sons.

Two more Ramirez bastards, Jake thought coldly.

And he'd left his fortune to be divided among the three of them.

"As if I'd touch a penny, you son of a bitch," Jake muttered through his teeth.

Should you wish to learn the identities of these men, the letter said, *Senhor Ramirez has stipulated a condition.*

A condition? Jake shot to his feet. If the SOB were alive, he'd fly to Brazil and tell him where to shove his condition.

He scanned the letter again. Ramirez had been guardian to some Brazilian kid. If he wished to learn the identities of the two other legatees Jake was to take over that role, be a kind of custodian to the child. Details would be forthcoming if he were interested.

"Interested?" Jake snorted. Right. That was just what he was in the mood for. Playing warden to some kid in another hemisphere.

He tossed the letter aside. To hell with the scum who'd sired him. To hell with conditions that were damned near demands from the grave. To hell with doing the bidding of the pig who'd never given a damn about him or his mother. And to hell with ever learning the names of his half-brothers. Because that was what they were. His half-brothers. The only other people on earth, aside from his mother, who shared his blood.

Jake stared at the letter once more. Then he cursed, folded it and put it in his pocket.

One thing he'd learned, building his empire. It was unwise to make important decisions in anger and just plain stupid to make them without gathering all the facts.

"Coffee's ready, Joaquim."

He'd make a couple of phone calls to this Javier Estes character. Or maybe he'd fly down to Rio, confront Estes in person. Yes. A face-to-face meeting might be best.

"Joaquim?"

"I'm on my way," he called.

Damned right, he was.

CHAPTER TWO

ACCORDING to its discreet brochure, the *Escola para Senhoritas Novas* lay nestled in the mountains a short drive from the city of Rio de Janeiro.

> *The school is near enough to Rio de Janeiro for our young ladies to benefit from the city's cultural opportunities, yet far enough from it to protect them from its temptations.*

The truth was that the School for Young Ladies, run by the Little Sisters of the Mountains, might as well have been located on Pluto. The nuns took girls with no demerits on their records to the opera at Teatro Municipal twice a year. Except for that, nothing that happened in Rio or in what the girls called "the real world" had any impact on the school.

Days began at six and ended at eight-thirty, when the lights in the stark dormitory rooms went out. Even the older girls, like Catarina, who had their own rooms—if you could call four cots jammed into a ten-by-twelve space one's own room—were forbidden to keep their lights on past nine.

No good had ever come of keeping late hours, Mother Elisabete told them.

She never said what benefit keeping early ones might bring.

Catarina had long ago figured out why the rules and the surroundings were so stark. The girls who boarded here during the week came from affluent homes; living a structured, even basic existence from Monday through Friday was expected to improve their character.

18

Curled in the window seat beside her cot, knees drawn to her chin as she gazed out at the dark night, Catarina Elena Teresa Mendes gave a deep, deep sigh.

The trouble was, Catarina lived that regimented existence seven days a week. Except for those twice a year trips to the theater, she'd never left the school in the eight years she'd been here.

You couldn't go home for the weekend when you had no home.

It was a warm night. Catarina had cracked the window an inch, which was as much against the rules as not being in bed at this hour, but she wanted to smell the flowers that grew wild in the courtyard below. Not even Mother Elisabete had been able to get rid of them. The elderly gardener would dig them up one week and they'd reappear the next.

Catarina was pretty sure he didn't really try very hard to kill the flowers. Once, when she'd walked by as he dug at them with a trowel, he'd looked up and closed one rheumy eye in a slow wink, as if to say that Mother Elisabete was powerful, but not powerful enough to destroy something as beautiful as a flower.

The flowers had a right to bloom. So did Catarina. Unfortunately, she didn't have anyone like the old gardener to make sure she got the chance.

She didn't hate the school, or the girls, or the Sisters for the limitations on her life. She didn't even hate Mother Elisabete who was, after all, only doing her job.

It was just that Mother's "job" was to be Catarina's keeper.

Catarina's long chestnut hair, free of its severely braided coronet only when she slept, tumbled down her back as she raised her eyes to the sky. On such a clear night, the stars seemed brighter than ever.

Maybe that was because of what lay ahead.

Maybe it was because of what would happen tomorrow, when she turned twenty-one.

Just thinking about it made Catarina tremble with excitement.

No more lights out at nine sharp. No more classes in such useless things as How To Arrange Flowers for a Dinner Party, interspersed with hours spent sneezing her way through the dusty files in Mother Elisabete's office.

"If we had a computer," she'd said, after a couple of weeks at the impossible task, "and a scanner, I could probably transfer all your files in a few days."

Stupid, stupid, stupid. Mother Elisabete had reacted as if she'd suggested inviting the devil to dinner.

"We need no modern temptations, Miss Mendes. And how do you know of such things in the first place?"

By reading magazines smuggled to her by the grocer's delivery boy, that was how. But admitting it would have led to trouble for the both of them.

"I just do," she'd said.

She'd been banished to her room each night after supper for the next two weeks. *Locked* in her room, as if she were twelve instead of almost twenty-one.

Catarina let out a breath.

Why dwell on the past? One more night, that was all, and she'd finally have back the freedom that had been taken from her at age thirteen, when her mother and father had died in a boating accident. An ancient great-uncle she'd never met had become her guardian, and he'd sent her to live at this school run by the Little Sisters of the Mountains.

At first, she'd been too wrapped in grief to question anything. She'd settled, numbly, into the school's routines. She watched girls reach the age of eighteen, graduate and leave. Five years after she'd first arrived, she'd waited with excitement for that glorious day.

"What will happen?" she'd asked Mother Elisabete.

"Will a car come for me? Will my great-uncle be in it? Where will I go?"

"Your uncle will come that day, yes," Mother Elisabete had replied. "He will explain everything."

Catarina had been thrilled to know she'd see her uncle a second time. Surely he was going to take her home, wherever that might be. The morning of her birthday, she almost trembled with excitement as he wobbled into Mother's office on a cane and sank into a chair.

"Uncle," Catarina said, "I'm very happy to see you."

The old man folded his hands around the golden head of his cane and told her that on her twenty-first birthday she would inherit a considerable fortune.

Then he told her the terms of that inheritance.

She had to remain here until she turned twenty-one.

The news had stunned her. Twenty-one? Surely eighteen was the age of majority in Brazil? Mother Elisabete had given her a stern look, no doubt because Catarina should not have possessed such worldly information. Her uncle had simply said yes, she was right, eighteen was the age of majority, but the will had been written when Brazilian law didn't always protect women. The stipulation about her remaining in the convent school, in the event of their deaths, had been her parents' attempt to safeguard her from unscrupulous suitors.

Catarina argued that the law had changed. It did offer women protection now.

"Perhaps," her uncle said, "but what has that to do with the terms of the will?"

The terms, he told her, were unalterable.

The law might have changed, but the will—and Catarina's life—had not.

Of course, she could always forfeit her inheritance.

Catarina knew better than to do that. Even at eighteen, cloistered in a place that might have seemed unchanged since colonial times, she understood that real freedom came with economic security, especially if you were female.

So she'd bitten back her disappointment, asked her uncle if he would look into the possibility of changing the will, even though he said it couldn't be done, and settled in for three more years spent learning little that would be of value in the real world.

The time crept by. Then, a few months ago, Mother Elisabete had summoned Catarina to her office again.

"There has been a change in your situation, Miss Mendes. I thought it best if you heard about it directly."

Catarina's pulse had quickened. Had her uncle finally found a way to set aside the terms of the will? She was fast approaching twenty-one, but even a few months off what she thought of as her sentence would have been a joy.

A white-haired man, not her uncle, was waiting for her with a solemn look on his face. His name, he said, was Javier Estes; he was her uncle's attorney. Her uncle had died. He paused; Mother Elisabete glared at her and Catarina realized she was expected to express her sorrow at the death of an old man she'd seen twice in her life.

"I'm saddened to hear it," she said, but her heart raced even faster. Did her uncle's death negate the terms of the will?

It did not. Javier Estes told her she was now the ward of a man named Enrique Ramirez. Regrettably, *Senhor* Ramirez was too old and too ill to visit her personally.

Nothing new there, Catarina had thought, but she'd nodded politely.

Estes told her that *Senhor* Ramirez wished to assure her that she was not to worry. Nothing would change. She'd go on living in the convent school until she was twenty-one...

And then she'd have two months to find a Brazilian husband her guardian would find suitable.

After that, she could claim her fortune.

Catarina felt the blood drain from her head. "What?" she'd said. "What?"

"Didn't your uncle mention this?"

"No. He didn't. And I don't believe it. It's not possible!"

Estes had pulled the will from his briefcase. He put on a pair of glasses, cleared his throat and read her the salient passages. Midway through, deaf to Mother Elisabete's hiss of outrage, Catarina snatched the document from the *advogado's* hands and read it for herself.

It was true. Not only did she have to be twenty-one to gain her inheritance, she had to be married to a "Brazilian her guardian finds suitable."

Catarina had lost all her composure. She'd argued. She'd raised her voice. She'd banged her fist on the desk. Estes shrugged and said there was nothing he could do about it; Mother Elisabete ordered her to her room.

"You cannot tell me what to do," Catarina had shrieked—but, of course, Mother could. Catarina wasn't alone in this: there were a handful of other girls at the convent school who'd stayed on well past their eighteenth birthdays. Some were happily studying all they could learn to become obedient wives; a couple of others were considering joining the Little Sisters.

Catarina wanted no part of either future. She wanted to live her own life.

She thought about running away, but she didn't have a *real* to her name. Besides, if she ran, she'd give up her inheritance, and she knew it was her ticket to the independence and freedom that had been stolen from her.

Now, finally, she was only one night from her twenty-first birthday. She'd be leaving this place. So far, though, Javier Estes hadn't contacted her.

Catarina caught her breath.

Maybe he wouldn't.

Maybe her birthday would arrive and she'd walk out the

gates a free woman. No more men dictating the terms of her existence, no more Mother Elisabete forcing adherence to the rigid code of an earlier century. Above all else, no more impossible stipulation that she marry a suitable Brazilian husband within two months.

Footsteps were coming down the hall. Catarina shut the window, climbed into bed and pulled the blanket to her chin before she realized she hadn't said her prayers.

She said them now. One prayer, anyway. A prayer to St. Teresa, her name saint, that her hopes for tomorrow might be realized.

She knew she ought to be satisfied with that, but Catarina's genes weren't one hundred percent Latin. Her mother had been a Boston-bred O'Brien. The nuns had done their best to make her forget that, but they hadn't succeeded.

It was the O'Brien in Catarina that added an earthy pledge to the prayer.

A suitable Brazilian husband? No way. She didn't plan on marrying anyone, let alone a horrible old man, which was what she knew those words meant.

Not even God would demand such a sacrifice.

Jake had never been to Rio before.

He'd read about it, knew that it was big, brassy and filled with contrasts, and, from the reactions of his fellow passengers in the American Airlines first-class cabin, he knew the approach over water had to be spectacular. But a glimpse of Sugar Loaf Mountain, another of waves breaking against the sand at Copacabana beach, and he lost interest.

He had a four o'clock appointment with Javier Estes. That was all he cared about. He'd get the names of his half-brothers—assuming Enrique's will hadn't been a lie—and head home.

Stepping out of the terminal was a shock. New York had been shivering in anticipation of an impending snowstorm.

Here, the temperature had to be at least ninety. The sun was so bright it was damned near blinding.

Jake took a taxi to his hotel, showered, changed clothes, downed two minuscule cups of thick, sweet Brazilian coffee in hopes the combination of caffeine and sugar would reverse the effects of the flight, and headed out the door. He could hardly wait to tell Estes what he could do with his dead client's insane demands.

Estes's secretary ushered him right into the attorney's office. Some of the wind went out of Jake's sails when he saw the man's age. It was hard to take an aggressive approach to somebody who looked old enough to be your grandfather. Worse, Estes began the discussion by saying he assumed Jake was angry and he could well understand the reason.

"I tried to convince him not to make such demands," Estes said, with a shake of his head, "but I am afraid your father was a very stubborn man."

"He wasn't my father," Jake said stiffly. "Not in any meaningful sense of the word."

Estes raised an eyebrow. "Some would say he was your father in the only meaningful sense of the word." He held up a hand before Jake could speak. "Let me be sure you understand what he has left to you. One third of a very considerable estate, and—"

"I don't want his money."

"And," Estes continued, "some information of a personal nature."

"The names of my half-brothers." Jake nodded. "That's the only reason I'm here."

"Then, I must ask you, *Senhor* Ramirez, are you prepared to meet the terms of the will?"

Jake sat back in his chair. "If you mean am I prepared to dance to a dead man's tune, the answer is no."

"I feared you would say that, *senhor*. Well, in that case,

our meeting is at an end.'' Estes began to get to his feet. ''I wish you a pleasant flight home, and—''

''I haven't come all this distance to turn tail and go home, *Senhor* Estes.''

''But you just said—''

''I want that information. I'll take you to court to get it.''

''The document is unbreakable.'' Estes smiled. ''I know that because I wrote it myself.''

''Does the name José Marin mean anything to you?''

''Of course. He is a fine lawyer.''

''Let's not play games, Estes. He's the best lawyer in Rio.''

''So some would say.''

''He will represent me.''

''He is very expensive.''

''And I am very rich,'' Jake said coldly.

Estes chuckled. ''Rich, and hard-headed. The same as your father.''

''I told you—''

''You will spend years trying to break this will, *senhor*, and you will not succeed. You will never know the names of your half-brothers. I regret this, but it is as your—as my client wished.''

Jake glared at the other man but he knew he was right. Even Marin had told him as much during the hour they'd talked on the phone yesterday.

Estes seemed to sense that Jake was weakening. ''How difficult could it be, *Senhor* Ramirez, to watch over this girl for two short months? She is a child, and she has spent eight years in a convent.''

''You've met her?''

''Certainly.''

''And?''

Estes mentally crossed his fingers. ''And she is what one would expect.'' It wasn't an out and out lie. The girl was precisely what one would expect, if one expected a spitfire mated to a whirlwind.

"If I were to agree," Jake said, emphasizing the "if," "what would I have to do? Pay her school bills? Send her birthday cards until she's eighteen? I have no idea what a guardian does."

"Well, for starters, you should know she already is eighteen."

Jake cocked his head. "She's eighteen? Then why does she need a guardian?"

"You won't be her guardian. Not exactly." Estes cleared his throat and reached into an open file drawer. "Perhaps it would be best if you read the pertinent clause yourself."

Jake narrowed his eyes. Things were more complicated than Estes wanted to admit. What was going on here?

"I'm American," he said coldly. "I don't read or speak Portuguese."

"I've had the document translated into English, *senhor*. Read it, please, and then we can talk."

Jake took the will. He read what Estes indicated. After a minute, he looked up.

"This is insane."

"I'm afraid not. *Senhor* Ramirez was perfectly competent when he insisted the clause giving you this responsibility be included in his will."

"The girl is twenty-one?"

"As of today, yes."

"And I'm supposed to…" Jake found the clause. "I'm supposed to 'nurture and protect her, introduce her to polite society and to men of good character and excellent means, and see to it that she marries such a man within two months'?" He stared at the lawyer. "Of course it's insane."

"It is the only means by which you will gain the information you want, *senhor*." Estes rose to his feet. "Shall we go to the convent so you can meet the girl?"

Jake flung Enrique's will to the floor. "I'd tell you where you can go," he said grimly, "except I know this is Enrique Ramirez's work, not yours. Goodbye, *Senhor* Estes."

"Good-day, *Senhor* Ramirez," Estes said.

He was already talking to an empty room—but Joaquim Ramirez would be back. Enrique had baited his trap well.

What man could resist the lure of discovering his true identity and his place in the world?

Less than three hours later, the two men were in a black SUV Jake had rented, approaching the closed iron gates of a building that looked like a medieval fortress.

"I am pleased you changed your mind," Estes said politely.

Jake grunted as he brought the SUV to a stop and beeped the horn. Changed his mind? That was a nice way of putting it. What else could he do? Rage had driven him from the *advogado*'s office. Common sense had brought him back.

A hand from the grave had him by the *cojones,* although that probably wasn't the right word in Portuguese.

Portuguese. Was that the only language the girl spoke? He hadn't thought to ask. He hadn't even asked Estes her name.

"Your ward's name," Estes said, as if he'd read Jake's mind, "is Catarina. Catarina Elena Teresa Mendes."

"Does she speak English?"

"I don't know."

That could be a problem, but he could always hire a translator. Jake tapped the horn again.

"And she understands what's going to happen? She accepts it? Because an American girl would laugh in your face if you told her she was going to be a stranger's ward for the two months it takes him to find her a husband."

"The girl has been raised as a Brazilian, not as an American."

"I know. I only meant— Well, never mind. She's accepted this, right?"

"I told you, she is precisely what one would expect her to be."

Jake nodded. He didn't like the trap he was in but at least Catarina Mendes wouldn't be a problem. He didn't know much about girls her age...

Well, yeah. He did. Samantha had just turned twenty-two. That was what the sapphire bracelet had been all about. But that was different. Sam was a woman of the world. For all intents and purposes, Catarina was still a child.

An old man tottered up to the gates, opened the lock and stepped aside. Jake gunned the engine, raised a plume of dust as he shot up the driveway, then stood on the brakes before a set of stone steps that led to a massive iron-bound door.

"This kid's lived in this place for eight years?"

"It's an excellent school," Estes said defensively.

At their knock, a wizened nun opened a small door set into the larger one and rattled off something to the attorney.

"The sister says Mother Elisabete is expecting us."

They made their way down a long, stone-walled corridor that glistened with damp. The air was cool even on this hot day. The lighting was poor and Jake almost missed the door that suddenly appeared before them. They were ushered into a room filled with heavy mahogany furniture. Dark draperies covered the windows.

The room's focal point was a massive desk. Behind it sat a thin-lipped woman in a black wimple and habit.

"Mother Elisabete," Estes said, "this is Joaquim Ramirez."

"*Senhor* Ramirez. A pleasure."

Jake doubted it. Mother Elisabete looked as if a smile would crack her face.

"Catarina," she said sharply. "Where are your manners? Stand and greet our visitors."

Jake hadn't even realized there was anyone else in the room until the nun barked the command. Now he saw a figure rise from a chair in the corner.

Yes, indeed.

An obedient mouse.

Catarina Elena Teresa Mendes, her head bowed, was tall and skinny, all but lost in the folds of an ugly brown dress that hung halfway to her ankles. Her face, what little he could see of it, was unremarkable. Her hair was mouse-brown and so tightly braided around her head that he half wondered if it wouldn't tug her eyes from their sockets.

Jake breathed a little easier. How tough would it be, watching over a girl like this? Finding her a suitable husband might be a little difficult, unless he could come up with a way to make her look a bit more attractive. From what he could see, that wasn't going to be easy, but her inheritance would help. He'd seen New York heiresses with looks that could stop a clock land outstanding husbands.

All he had to do was contact a few people and— Damn, in his anger, he'd all but forgotten that he knew a guy at the Brazilian Embassy. Not well—they'd met at a couple of charity dinners, played a little racquetball—but in New York that was enough reason to phone him, invite him for a drink, tell him about Catarina, get her invited to a few parties.

Jake felt his remaining tension drain away. He'd fly home tonight, arrange for an apartment for the girl, hire a companion to watch over her, phone Lucas and get things moving.

"Miss Mendes," he said pleasantly. The mouse didn't respond. She didn't even look up. Jake raised his eyebrows. "Does she speak English?"

Estes and Mother Elisabete engaged in some rapid-fire Portuguese. Then the nun shrugged her shoulders.

"Very little, I am afraid. But rest assured, *Senhor* Ramirez, Catarina understands what is expected of her and she will be most cooperative. Isn't that right, Catarina?"

A jerk of the head, though the girl's eyes were still downcast. At least she'd understood enough English for that. Silence descended on the room. Jake cleared his throat. He felt like an idiot…or like a man buying a car. Was he supposed to say something in lieu of kicking the tires?

"I assume you have an appropriate place for her to live, *Senhor* Ramirez?"

Not yet, but why mention that? The sooner he got this idiotic scheme rolling, the sooner he could say goodbye to Catarina Mendes and hello to the two strangers who were his brothers.

"*Senhor?*"

"Yes," he said firmly, "of course."

Mother Elisabete nodded and rose to her feet. "In that case, you may take her."

Jake blinked. "Now?"

"Now. She is twenty-one today. We don't have facilities for girls older than that."

"I see." Jake cleared his throat again. "Well, then, Miss Mendes? *Senhor* Estes? Shall we—?"

"I'm staying for dinner," Estes said hurriedly. "Mother and I have things to discuss. I'll take a taxi back to town."

Jake nodded. It looked as if he was on his own with the mouse. "Uh, if you'd tell Miss Mendes that, uh, that it's time for her to leave…"

The girl reached for a leather satchel behind her chair. He reached for it, too, and their hands brushed. She jerked her hand from his as if she'd been burned.

Jake smiled politely. "Sorry."

The girl mumbled something in Portuguese. Mother Elisabete hissed; Estes made a choking sound. Why? Were they both that surprised the girl would apologize? That was what it had been, wasn't it? An apology? What else would such a docile child offer in such a difficult situation?

Estes shook his hand, said something to the girl. So did Mother Elisabete. The girl never raised her eyes, not even after the same nun who'd admitted them walked them to the front door and shut it behind them.

Jake tossed the girl's satchel in the back of the SUV and opened her door. She got in, strapped on her seat belt, all without saying a word or looking at him. Poor kid. She was probably terrified.

He waited until they were speeding along the narrow road that led down the mountain.

"Miss Mendes. I know this must all seem strange…"

No answer. No flick of her head in his direction.

"We're going to Rio. To my hotel."

Still no response. He could hardly blame her.

"Tomorrow we'll fly to the United States. I'll find an apartment for you to stay in for the next two months, arrange for a companion…" Nothing. Not even a nod of her head. Did she understand a word he was saying? "Miss Mendes. Catarina. I don't know how much English you understand, but—"

"I speak English fluently."

Whoops. Catarina grabbed the door handle as the SUV swerved. Her new guardian—her jailer—recovered control of the wheel quickly enough so that they didn't go over the precipice, but it was close.

Perhaps she should have been more cautious in telling him she wasn't the idiot he obviously thought she was.

"You do?" he said, his voice rising in disbelief.

Catarina smoothed down her skirt. "English is the *lingua franca* of the world."

She felt him looking at her, though she knew he wouldn't be able to see her any more clearly than she could see him. The sun was almost gone; they were both in shadow. But what did it matter how he looked? She had to go with him, even if he turned out to be a clone of the Hunchback of Notre Dame.

Mother Elisabete had told her the facts. *Senhor* Joaquim Ramirez wanted no part of her. He'd been forced to take on her guardianship now that the older Ramirez was dead, and unless she was very careful he would not go through with it, in which case she'd have to remain at the School for Young Ladies while the attorney figured out what to do next, and who knew how much longer that might take?

She hadn't even intended to speak to the man until they were safely away from the convent, but impatience had gotten the better of her. He talked to her as if she were a child and she was sick and tired of that.

"Besides," she added, "my mother was American. We spoke both English and Portuguese at home."

"I see," Joaquim Ramirez said, although she suspected he didn't. "Well. That will definitely make things eas—"

"There's a turn-off ahead. Pull over so we can talk." A mistake. She knew it as soon as she said it. Nice little convent-bred girls didn't give orders. "I mean…" She took a breath, dropped her voice to a whisper. "Please. This has all been such a shock… Can't we just discuss things for a little while?"

She saw his hands flex on the wheel. Then he put on his signal light and pulled to the side of the road.

"Look," he said, swinging toward her, "I don't know what's going on here, but you're right. I'm not in the mood for this deal, either, but there's a will, Miss Mendes. Estes says he explained its terms to you and you accepted them."

"I didn't! Nobody gave me a choice. That's what I'm trying to—"

Her words were lost in the grinding gears of an eighteen-wheeler as it labored up the steep road. Illumination from its headlights filled the car.

And Jake got a clear look at Catarina Mendes for the very first time.

She was beautiful.

Her face wasn't bony, it was elegant. Straight nose. High cheekbones. Determined chin. Eyes the color of dark coffee, a mouth that was rosy-pink and generous, innocent of make-up. Innocent, too, he was certain, of a man's taste.

His eyes dropped lower. That brown thing she was wearing was still ugly and oversized, but because of the way she'd shifted in her seat, because of the pressure of her seat belt, he could see that she had a slender neck, delicate shoulders, and the sensual promise of lush, rounded breasts.

Jake felt a tightening in his groin. Where had his demure little mouse gone?

"I know the terms of my parents' will," Catarina said. "Do you really want to force me to follow them? To see me wed a man I don't love?"

He lifted his gaze to meet hers. Her cheeks were flushed; her dark eyes were bright with unshed tears. She put her hand on his arm and leaned closer, her mouth trembling.

"All you need do is take me to Rio and lend me enough money to live on for the next two months. At the end of that time, you can contact Javier Estes and tell him I'm safely married. I'll come into my inheritance, pay you what I owe you, and nobody will be the wiser."

"Miss Mendes. I wish I could do that, but Estes will demand proof."

"You can find a way. I know you can."

Was she wearing perfume? She couldn't be. Was that the smell of flowers blooming in the darkness that now surrounded them, or was that her scent teasing his senses?

"Please," she whispered, "I beg you. Help me."

He wanted to. What man wouldn't? Maybe what she'd suggested would work. Drop her off in Rio, give her some money, wait a while, then contact Estes and somehow convince him he'd complied with the terms of the will...

And maybe he'd lost his mind. There was no way to fool Javier Estes. He had to make her understand that.

"*Senhor?* Will you help me?"

Jake cleared his throat. "I wish I could, but—"

"How much is Estes paying you?"

The sharp words matched her demeanor, which had changed in a heartbeat. Her eyes were still bright, but now it was with the flare of anger. She snatched back her hand as if touching him was the same as touching a maggot.

Jake's eyes narrowed. "Do you think I'd do this for money?"

"How much?" she repeated. "Tell me, and I'll double it."

In that instant, he realized he'd been snookered. This was no sweetly obedient mouse; this was a woman. Mother Elisabete and Javier Estes had tossed him a hot potato.

His first instinct was to turn the SUV around and take Catarina Mendes back to the convent. *No way,*, he'd say. You want to find the lady a husband, do it yourself.

And then what would he do? Return to Rio? Tell Marin he wanted to go to court even though he knew he didn't have a chance in hell of breaking the airtight provisions of the will?

Spend the rest of his life wondering if every dark-haired man who bore even the slightest resemblance to him might also carry his blood?

"Not enough?" Catarina lifted her chin. "I'll pay you triple whatever—"

"I told you, I'm not doing this for money."

"I don't believe you! Why else would—?"

She gasped as his hands closed on her shoulders. "Nobody can buy me, Miss Mendes," Jake said coldly. "You'd better get that through your head right now. I'm going to do what I have to do. The sooner you accept that, the better.''

Her eyes narrowed; a Portuguese word he didn't understand hissed from her lips. Jake smiled grimly.

''Whatever you just called me was right on the mark. I am a son of a bitch, a hard-nosed bastard, your worst nightmare come true—you name it. You will live where I put you for the next two months, you will behave as I instruct, you will curb that nasty tongue and charm the men I introduce you to, and you will marry one of them when I tell you to. Do you understand?''

She understood, all right. Mother Elisabete and the attorney had handed her over to a monster. He didn't look like one—her jailer was young and handsome—but nobody ever said monsters had to be ugly on the outside.

Somehow, that only made things seem worse.

His life stretched ahead of him.

All that stretched ahead of her was whatever he would force upon her.

She felt the hot prick of tears and blinked them back. She would not cry. She hadn't cried since they'd told her she'd lost her parents. Tears were a sign of weakness. If she'd learned nothing else at the School for Young Ladies, she'd learned that. Still, she couldn't keep her voice from wobbling.

''You're going to regret this, *Senhor* Ramirez.''

Jake already did, but why give her the satisfaction of admitting it? Instead, he gave her a look meant to tell her that nothing she could say or do would affect him.

Big mistake.

Her hair had come loose from the pins that held it and fell around her face in waves. An image of himself putting his hands in her hair, winding the length around his fist as he drew her toward him and took that soft-looking, innocent mouth with his, flashed through his mind.

Jake pulled back, put the car in gear and drove for Rio as if the devil were on his tail.

CHAPTER THREE

JAKE pulled up to his hotel the same way he'd pulled up to the gates of the school, so fast and hard the tires of the SUV screamed in complaint.

If only he could get out of Rio and this nightmare the same way. Go straight to the airport, leave the selfish demands of the man who'd sired him behind, leave the burden of being guardian to Catarina Mendes behind, pick up the pieces of his life and forget everything that had happened since the arrival of the letter.

But he couldn't. Learning who his brothers were, finding them, discovering what they were like, was becoming the most important thing in his life.

Were they facing challenges as unwanted as his in order to unravel the secrets Enrique had taken to his grave?

Maybe it was foolish, but thinking they were gave him the determination he needed to propel him out of the SUV and to the passenger side where his ward sat, as unmoving as a statue.

He got there just as the valet reached him.

"*Senhor,*" the boy said politely.

Jake yanked open the door. Catarina was all but wedged against it, her window wide open. She'd put it down long before they'd reached the city, even though he'd had the a/c going full blast, as if to get rid of a bad smell. Him, probably. He'd decided to let her drag in the jet stream if it would keep her silent.

The wind had not been kind. It had whipped her hair into a thousand wild strands until she looked like a stand-in for Medusa.

38

No problem there. It went well with the shapeless brown thing that encased her.

Jake waited for her to acknowledge his presence. She didn't and he leaned toward her. The valet was just behind him. No reason to turn this into performance art, he thought, and spoke quietly.

"Out of the car, Miss Mendes."

Except for a slight twitch of her mouth, she didn't move.

The hard way, then, Jake thought, and leaned in closer.

"I said, get out."

Catarina looked at him, looked past him, and rattled off something in Portuguese. Jake turned around in time to see the valet's face turn white. Not a good sign, he thought coldly.

"What did she say?"

The valet's Adam's apple bobbed up and down. "I do not—I am not sure—"

Jake straightened up, blocked Catarina from the guy's view and forced a smile.

"Tell me what the lady said."

"She said—the *senhorita* said… She said you have abducted her, *senhor*."

Jake shut his eyes and took a deep breath before opening them again and reading the brass name tag pinned to the valet's maroon and gold jacket.

"Andres," he said, his tone confidential, "I am afraid we have a problem."

"We do?"

"*Sim*. Yes." He took Andres by the elbow and walked him a couple of feet away. "You see, the lady—the *senhorita*—is not well."

Color crept back into the valet's face. "Ah," he said, peering past Jake.

"In fact, one look at her and I'm sure you can see just how ill she is."

The valet rose on his toes and took another look.

Jake was confident he knew what his reaction would be. Rio was a city of incredibly beautiful women; this was one of its finest hotels. He'd have bet his last *real* the valet had never before encountered a female guest who seemed to be wearing a fright wig and a burlap sack.

The boy turned his attention back to Jake. "I do see, yes, *senhor*. So sad. She is young to be so, um, so…"

"Exactly."

"I am sorry for your—for your—"

"Niece," Jake said quickly. "Thank you. Yes. It's truly unfortunate." He dug several bills from his pocket and stuffed them into the valet's hand. "If you would be so kind as to inform the staff not to pay attention to any, uh, any disturbances my, uh, my niece might create this evening…"

The valet nodded. "I will tell them, *senhor*."

"Thank you, Andres. Sometimes my, ah, my niece becomes agitated. When she does… Well, I'm sure you understand."

"Certainly. If I can do anything to help…"

You could, but only if you knew a way to rip Enrique Ramirez from the grave, Jake thought grimly. But he smiled like the benevolent uncle he was supposed to be, gave a sad shake of his head and said he would do his best to manage alone. His niece was less likely to be a problem that way. Then he went back to the vehicle, wrapped his hand around Catarina's wrist and brought his mouth close to her ear.

"Here's the deal," he said coldly. "You can walk into the hotel on your own, or I'll sling you over my shoulder and carry you. Take it or leave it."

Her chin went up a notch.

"Do it. The *policia* will be here before you can blink."

"That's fine. I can explain the same thing to them I've already explained to the valet. They'll be most sympathetic to a man who must deal with a niece who suffers from hallucinations.'' A tight smile curved his mouth. ''They'll probably even help me find a psychiatric hospital in which I can place you until our flight leaves.''

That made her look at him, all right.

''You wouldn't dare!''

''Try me.''

Catarina stared at him. A shudder went through her.

''Why are you doing this?''

Jake opened her seat belt. ''Get out of the car, Catarina.''

''If it isn't for money…''

''I'm going to count to three.''

''Are you related to Enrique Ramirez? You have the same name.''

''One.''

''Was he your father? Did you love him so much that you would do his bidding even after his death?''

''Two.''

''What kind of man would consent to such an awful demand? Don't you have a mind of your own?''

''Three,'' Jake said, and reached for her.

''All right!'' She jerked away from his hand. ''I'll get out. Just don't touch me.''

He stood aside and Catarina stepped from the car and swept past him, spine straight, head high, even though she was ready to weep with frustration. And fear. Fear that had become so powerful during the last part of the drive into town it had almost suffocated her.

She'd been so horrified by the knowledge that she would be married off to a stranger that she hadn't let herself think about what had just happened.

A strange man all but owned her.

''*Senhorita*,'' the valet said, flashing a smile so patently false she knew Ramirez must have told him something truly awful.

The doorman snapped to attention, the glass door swung wide, and Catarina entered the hotel.

Her captor was right on her heels.

"Captor" was the right word for this man, who obviously had no heart, no conscience, no sense of human decency. She'd been wrong, saying he could be led around. Nobody would lead him anywhere he didn't want to go, this Joaquim Ramirez or Jake Ramirez, whatever he called himself.

He was *macho. Muito macho.*

On top of that, he was beautiful.

Maybe that was the wrong word to describe a man, but she couldn't think of another that came close. She'd stolen a long look at him from beneath her lashes when they were in Mother Elisabete's office. Just for a moment, before they'd told her who he was and what he was going to do with her, she'd conjured up a fantasy about a black-haired, green-eyed knight come to save her from the dragon.

What a shock to find out that the knight *was* the dragon.

Now she wondered what other things she would learn about him. He'd taken her to Rio. To this hotel, glittering with lights and almost smelling of sin. Wicked places both, or so other girls had whispered late at night, after the lights were out.

They'd whispered other things, too.

What would happen to her once she and Joaquim Ramirez were alone?

From the corner of her eye, she saw the parking valet dart toward the reception desk. Catarina looked over at the clerk behind it just as the valet stepped close and whispered in his ear. The clerk darted a look at her, then looked away.

Coward, Catarina thought, but she had to admit her captor's story was more convincing than her own.

Suddenly, Ramirez was beside her. He curled his hand around her elbow. She jumped at the touch and his fingers bit into her skin.

''Behave yourself,'' he said softly.

The elevator bank was straight ahead. Guests were stepping from one of the cars. Women wearing tiny dresses, little more than an arrangement of scarves. High heels that made their hips swing when they walked. Was that why they clutched the arms of the men who escorted them? Why they draped themselves over them, hip to hip, thigh to thigh?

They stared at her. Catarina stared back. She couldn't believe what she saw. Those dresses, so low at the bodice, so high at the hem, made her blush.

Her undergarments were less revealing.

Whispers, little smiles of amusement, raised eyebrows. She felt her face heat. She knew how she looked. No make-up—cosmetics weren't permitted at the convent school. No artfully styled hair. That wasn't permitted, either. And this dress, this mud-colored thing she'd made in sewing class...

She could almost hear the buzz. What was she doing with a man whose looks put all these other men's looks to shame?

It was a good question.

The elevator starter greeted her captor by name. The doors whisked open; Ramirez drew her into the car and they rose to the top floor in silence. Once there, he marched her down the carpeted corridor toward a pair of double doors at the end.

''It isn't necessary to drag me.''

To her horror, her voice trembled. She turned the tremor into a cough.

She had to walk quickly to keep up with his long stride. At school, she'd been one of the tallest girls. She'd towered over the few men who passed through the gates but she barely came up to her captor's shoulder. She had to look up to see his face and she didn't like that. It made her feel overpowered.

''I said—''

"I heard what you said." A dip of the key-card and the doors swung open. Catarina didn't move and he put his hand in the small of her back and propelled her into the room. Once the door was closed, locked and bolted, he switched on the lights. A chandelier that looked almost as big as her convent bedroom blazed to life.

They were in a sitting room so lush it made her breath catch. Flowers spilled from vases on all the tables; the wall of windows revealed Rio wearing a queen's ransom in a necklace of light.

"Okay," Ramirez said, "let's get a few things straight."

He stood in the center of the room, arms folded, eyebrows knotted in a dark scowl. Catarina blinked and focused on him. He looked huge and almost overwhelmingly male.

Don't let anyone ever know that you're scared. It was a philosophy that had served her well during the first awful months following the deaths of her parents, but her bravado was fast crumbling under the toll of the endless day.

"You've already gotten a few things straight," she said, trying for sarcasm and not at all sure she'd achieved it. "You're in charge and I'm expected to obey."

"I'm in charge, as you put it, because your parents wanted it that way."

"They did not!" A surge of anger lent vibrancy to her voice. "They left me in the care of my uncle."

"Yes." His mouth seemed to soften. "And then you lost him, too. I'm sure it was quite a blow."

The "blow", as he'd put it, came of what had happened today, but why tell him that and lose some slight edge?

"It was. He was family."

"And I'm not."

"No." Her head came up. "I don't even know who you are."

"I told you. I'm—"

"I don't mean that. I mean, I don't know anything about you."

His teeth showed in a mirthless grin. "Then we're even."

"That's not true. You knew where we were going when we left the convent. You know where we're going after this. You knew you were going to control my destiny while I thought I'd be free." Her voice shook. *Damn it, Catarina!* she thought, and swallowed hard. "At least tell me why you've agreed to this—this impossible arrangement."

It was, Jake knew, a question she was entitled to ask. Her parents, fate and the damnable Enrique Ramirez had put her life in his hands. She'd put up a good front so far, but he was pretty sure a front was all it was. The tremor in her voice, the stripes of color across her cheeks that only emphasized her pallor, were dead giveaways.

Catarina Mendes had been whisked from the only home she knew, handed to a stranger, told that he controlled her existence even though she was of age, even though she was a woman...

Never mind that.

She was scared, and he couldn't blame her. Maybe it was time to regroup.

"Miss Mendes," Jake said gently, "why don't you sit down?"

"I don't need to sit."

"Maybe not, but I sure do. It's been a long day. I'm tired, irritable, and now that I think about it, I'm starved." He reached for the phone. "What would you like?"

"My freedom," she said, "that's what I'd like."

He nodded. "Yes. I'm sure you would. But—"

"But you're not about to let me have it."

"It's not as simple as you'd like to make it sound."

"It is," she said, on a hint of desperation. "All you have to do is tell that attorney you've decided to step aside."

"Okay. Let's assume I said, sure, go ahead, you want to

take off? Go on. Do it.'' Jake tucked his hands in his trouser pockets and leaned a hip against the sofa. "What would happen next?"

"What do you mean, what would happen next? I'd be free."

"Free? You'd be all alone in a city that can be as cruel as it is beautiful, sleeping in the streets, at the mercy of everyone who saw you. Does that sound like freedom to you?"

"I'd manage," Catarina said, even though her stomach lurched at the thought of the abyss he'd so accurately described.

"I don't think so. Besides, you've left something out. The most important item. You wouldn't get your inheritance."

"That's not true. I'll get a lawyer. He'll understand that my parents never meant my life to be handed over to a stranger."

"You're right, I'm sure they didn't."

"You see? Even you have to admit the truth. Once I have a lawyer, he'll contact Javier Estes, demand a change in the terms of my parents' will and— Have I said something amusing, *senhor?*"

"I'm not laughing at you," Jake said carefully. "I'm laughing at myself. Just a day or two ago, I thought the same thing. I'd get a lawyer, he'd handle Estes and, *pow,* I'd be out of the picture." His smile faded. "I was wrong. There's no way out of this. We're trapped. The will your parents wrote is airtight. So is the will my—" He caught himself. "So is the will that involves me."

She stared at him, her eyes wide and shiny with tears he knew she didn't want to shed.

"Why should I believe you?"

"Because I'm telling you the truth. Believe me, I'd love it if you were right. You think I'm looking forward to this?"

She didn't answer. Jake couldn't blame her. Why should

she see the situation from his point of view when, to her way of thinking, he didn't see it from hers?

"Look," he said carefully, "it's been a rough day. Here's what I suggest." He jerked his head toward one of a pair of closed doors. "There are two bedrooms. You take that one. It has a private bath. Why don't you wash up, maybe take a shower?" He glanced at the satchel he'd taken from the car. It seemed far too small to hold all her possessions but he had the feeling it did. "Change into something that's more comfortable than that, ah, that dress you're wearing, if you like."

"What's wrong with this dress?" Her jaw shot forward. "I made it myself."

"Really? That's, um, that's…" Jake cleared his throat. "Go on. Freshen up while I order dinner."

Dinner. Just the word made her salivate, but Catarina would sooner have starved than admit it.

"Don't bother. I'm not hungry."

"Yeah, but I am. You don't want to eat, that's fine. You can watch me pack away enough for the both of us."

She'd have told him she had no interest in watching him do anything but exit her life, except he reached for the phone at the same time he shrugged off his suit jacket.

Padding, she'd told herself, that was what made his shoulders seem so wide.

Not true. They were like that all on their own.

He had on a pale blue shirt, spun of the kind of fine cotton that felt like silk. She knew about such things, thanks to Sister Elberta's Home Economics class.

"*How will you properly furnish your husband's elegant home if you don't know how to make the correct choices in materials?*" the Sister said.

Catarina had tuned out. Who cared about the differences between Egyptian cotton and Indian cotton? One looked the same as another, draped over a chair.

Things changed when a fabric was draped over a man.

"Room Service?" Ramirez said into the phone. "Do you speak…? Good. Great. I'd like to order…"

She didn't hear the rest. How could she concentrate when he had the audacity to start undressing as if she weren't there? The nerve! she thought, as he undid his cuffs and rolled them back. Not that it mattered. She'd seen a man's arms before. The old gardener sometimes rolled back his sleeves when he…

Her breath caught.

The gardener's arms were ropy and wizened.

Her guardian's were a golden tan, hard with muscle and lightly dusted with fine black hair.

Now he was peeling off his tie. *Wait a minute,* she wanted to say, *can't you see I'm still standing here?* Instead, she stared, transfixed, as he opened first the top button of his shirt, then the next two. Three. Four.

His throat was a tanned corded column, leading down to a flat, muscled chest. Still talking, he started tugging his shirt from his trousers.

"Yes," he said. "Right. A pot of coffee. American coffee. And a glass of milk—"

Catarina saw a silky arrow of dark hair, a flat belly, that arrow of hair again…

He swung toward her. She looked up, their eyes met, and she turned on her heel and fled into the bedroom.

Jake heard the sound of the shower.

Once he did, he headed for his room.

Catarina could be playing games. She might have turned on the water to fool him. Even now, for all he knew, she could be huddled on the other side of the bedroom door, just waiting to make a break for freedom.

Maybe that would be for the best.

That expression on her face a few minutes ago, as if she'd seen... What? A ghost? A monster?

A man.

It was a safe bet she'd just experienced a first. A half-naked man. Well, not that he'd actually been half naked, but...

But that look in her eyes. Not fear, exactly. More like—like wonder. Curiosity. As if she were trying to imagine how it would feel to touch a man's skin. Run her hand over his chest. Feel the difference between his hardness and her softness.

Because she would be soft, under that ugly dress.

She would be silk and satin, all warm golden skin that had never known a man's caress. Breasts that had never been cupped by a man's hands. Nipples that had never felt the whisper of a man's tongue or the heat of his breath.

Jake shuddered, wiped the crazy images from his head, pulled off the rest of his clothes and got into the shower.

Minutes later, restored to sanity, wearing a pair of old grey sweatpants and a washed-out University of Michigan T-shirt, he strolled into the sitting room. His ward's door was still shut.

Of course that didn't mean she was still behind it.

Stupid to have left her unattended, he thought grimly...but the door that led from the suite to the hall was still bolted. Unless his charge had learned how to slip out through the keyhole, she was—

The door to her room opened. Jake swung around.

Catarina Mendes stood in the doorway. The ugly brown thing was gone, replaced by a long white nightgown over which she wore a white terrycloth hotel robe. From her little gasp of breath, he figured she hadn't expected to find him in the sitting room, and she fumbled for the robe's sash, brought the ends together and hurriedly knotted them. But not before Jake made some observations.

The first was that the nightgown was designed to be as sexless, as unfeminine as possible.

He swallowed dryly.

The second was that things didn't always play out as intended. The plain, unsexy gown clung to her body in all the places it shouldn't. He could see an outline of long, endless legs, rounded breasts and pebbled nipples.

"Oh," she said.

Oh, indeed.

Jake swallowed dryly and dragged his gaze to her face. It didn't help, not when she stared at him through darkly lashed eyes that held all the fear and vulnerability she'd done such a fine job of hiding until now; not when her newly washed hair fell to her shoulders in the chestnut and gold of an autumn woods.

Looking down didn't do any good, either. Which made no sense because all he could see were her bare toes peeping out from beneath the hem of the nightgown. He wasn't into feet—well, not unless they were encased in sky-high Manolos—so how come those toes, free of stilettos and even of polish, were having an effect on his hormones?

"I—I didn't realize…"

Jake bit back a groan. "No," he said, "neither did I."

He knew they were talking about two different things, but hell, he was lucky he could talk at all—luckier still when a knock at the door signaled the arrival of Room Service.

"Coming," he called, wincing at his bad choice of response, wincing that he should even be thinking such a thing…

Wincing because he knew it was time to stop kidding himself.

His ward, his charge, his unasked-for burden—whatever you wanted to call Catarina Mendes—was no child.

She was a woman, a gorgeous woman, untouched, unawakened, unexplored. He was charged with spending the next two months protecting her from the temptations of a century she wouldn't recognize and from the men who'd surely come running when they saw her.

He would have to select one of those men to marry her.

To take her innocence.

To carry Catarina Mendes to his bed.

The knock at the door sounded again. Jake gave himself a little shake and opened it.

"Good evening, sir. I have your order here."

No. He hadn't ordered any of it. The woman, the will...

"Sir?"

"Yeah," Jake said gruffly, and stepped aside.

CHAPTER FOUR

CATARINA had sworn she wouldn't take a forkful.

She didn't. She took shovelfuls.

Not right away, of course. First, she just stood by and watched as Jake pulled up a chair, uncovered half a dozen silver serving dishes, made a couple of appreciative umms and hmms and began heaping things on his plate.

By the time he'd tucked into what looked like a mushroom and cheese omelet, her belly was making unladylike noises. She colored, sure he could hear them, but he said nothing. He didn't even look at her.

Was he going to eat everything in sight?

Catarina yanked out a chair and sat down opposite him. Jake picked up a plate, filled it and held it out.

"Thank you," she said coldly, and took it.

God, she was starved! The omelet was wonderful. Mushroom and cheese, but there was bacon in it, too. The delicately fried potatoes were to die for, and the salad had something in the dressing—coconut?—that made each mouthful ambrosia.

She ate everything he'd served her plus two slices of buttered toast and a wedge of cheese. When he reached beneath the serving cart and produced a tulip glass filled with vanilla ice cream topped with strawberries, she vowed not to touch it. There was only the one serving; it was meant for her, and she knew it was the kind of treat an adult would order for a child.

The sooner he understood she wasn't a child, the better.

But it looked so delicious, that cool mountain of vanilla. More than that, ice cream was a rare treat. Dessert at school had consisted of grainy puddings and stewed-to-the-point-of-death fruit.

Surely one mouthful wouldn't hurt.

One. And then another and another. Before she knew it, the spoon clattered against the bottom of the glass. She twirled it around, captured the final sweet drops, licked them from the bowl of the spoon with the tip of her tongue...

And looked up and saw Jake watching her with burning eyes.

Something happened deep, deep in her belly. Heat, swift and sudden. Heat that spread through her blood, to her breasts.

Catarina's breath caught. The spoon rattled against her plate. She broke eye contact and patted her lips with her napkin. When she looked up again, she knew she'd been hallucinating.

There was nothing in her guardian's eyes but faint amusement.

"Feeling better?"

"It's important to take proper nourishment," she said stiffly.

A smile played at the corner of his mouth. "Words of wisdom from Mother Elisabete?"

"I don't appreciate being made fun of, *senhor*."

Jake pushed his plate away and reached for the coffee pot. "I'm not making fun of you, *senhorita*, I'm simply commenting on what I observed today." He filled a cup with the steaming black liquid and began lifting it to his lips.

"I'd like some coffee, too."

"You?"

"Me."

"You're too..."

Too what? Too young for caffeine? Not if he was right

about what he'd seen a moment ago. That sudden awareness of the way he'd been looking at her...

No. Forget that. The rush of color in her face, the way she'd parted her lips, the swift rise of her breasts, hadn't meant a thing. And if seeing her lick the last bit of ice cream from that spoon had almost driven him out of his mind, that was his problem, not hers.

Catarina Mendes might be of legal age but she was just a kid. She was his ward.

It would be unwise to forget that.

"Do they let you have coffee at the convent?"

"No," she said unhesitatingly, "but you've made it quite clear I'm not at the convent any more." She plucked a cup and saucer from the table and held them out. "Coffee, if you please, *Senhor* Ramirez."

Jake tightened his jaw, picked up the pot and poured.

"Was I right?"

"About what?"

"About you getting words of wisdom from Mother Elisabete. I got the feeling she was filled with advice for her charges."

"She means well."

"I'm sure she does."

"She looks out for her girls, and—" And what? Catarina frowned. Why was she saying these things? Mother Elisabete might be an excellent administrator but nobody, not even the nuns, would ever say she looked out for the girls. There wasn't much sense in automatically contradicting everything Ramirez said. "Actually," she said primly, "we learned about nourishment in Health Class."

"Ah. Health 101. Let's see... The food pyramid. A sound mind in a sound body. The value of exercise and of drinking eight glasses of water a day."

He sounded serious but there was that hint of laughter again. It put little crinkles at the corners of his eyes.

Such green eyes. Deep, deep emerald...

"And sex."

Catarina blinked. "Excuse me?"

"I was thinking about the topics we covered when I took Health."

"You must have a good memory," she said sweetly, and was pleased to see it was his turn to blush.

"I'm thirty. Not exactly ancient, Miss Mendes."

Thirty. She'd been trying to figure out his age. He was the youngest man she'd spoken to since she'd gone to live at the convent.

"Anyway, I'd bet the health curriculum hasn't changed all that much." He sipped at his coffee, his gaze steady on hers above the thin rim of his cup. "So, what about it?"

"What about what?"

"Did your Health Class include sex education?"

She could feel her cheeks burning. "No."

He sighed, as if she'd just placed the woes of the world at his feet.

"No. I didn't think it would."

"And," she said, with enough aplomb to have delighted the sister who taught Deportment, "it is not a proper topic for us to discuss."

A muscle knotted in his jaw. "If you're going to marry in two months, it is."

Catarina jerked back in her chair. Jake could have happily cut out his tongue, but it was too late.

"I'm sorry," he said. "Damn it, I didn't mean to be so blunt, but—"

But he had spoken the truth. For a little while she'd almost forgotten why she was here. The elegant suite, the delicious meal, the male-female banter with the incredibly gorgeous man seated across from her, had blinded her to reality.

She'd almost forgotten that all this was an illusion.

The hotel was only a more gilded prison than the one where she'd spent most of her life. The food was meant to lull her into complacent acceptance. And the man who looked like he'd stepped from a dream had no heart.

How could she have forgotten?

"Catarina."

His expression was so earnest she longed to wipe it from his face.

"Catarina, listen to me. Your life is about to change. Don't you want to talk about some of those changes before they occur?"

"I am not," she said, her tone venomous, "going to talk about sex with you."

Hell. He didn't want to talk about sex with her, either. He wasn't even sure how he'd come to bring up the topic but now that he had, okay, why not get it over with? He had to know what she knew. What she didn't know. Because she didn't, he thought grimly, know the first damned thing about what went on between men and women.

"You'll have to talk with someone. You can't just… I can't just let you…" Jake said a word that made her eyes widen. "You think this is easy for me? It isn't. It's an enormous responsibility."

"All you have to do is find a man who'll be willing to take me as his wife and your so-called responsibility will be over."

"The right man."

"Oh, of course. Sorry. I forgot. A proper Brazilian husband." Her mouth trembled. "That should be easy enough when you dangle my inheritance under his nose."

"Goddamnit," Jake said sharply. He rose from the table. "Do you really think I'd hand you over to just anyone?"

"You're shouting."

"Damned right I'm shouting!" He took a deep breath. "Look. None of this was my idea. I have a life. A life I made for myself. A life I enjoy.'' The chair he'd sat on was in his way. He kicked it aside and stalked across the room. ''And now I'm knee-deep in *your* life, and I don't like it.''

''Is that why we're flying to your country tomorrow?''

''You make it sound as if we're flying to Mars.''

''I don't have a passport,'' Catarina said, with the desperation of a woman grasping at a straw that might keep her from being swept downstream.

Jake looked at her. ''Yeah, you do.''

''I do?''

''Estes gave me some papers. Your birth certificate, your graduation diploma, your passport and visa.''

''But—but I don't want to...'' Catarina heard the mounting panic in her voice and took a deep breath. So far she was certain she'd managed to keep from showing how terrified she was. It was all the protection she had. ''I don't see why you're taking me to the United States. If I have to find a—a suitable Brazilian husband, this is the place to do it.''

''I'm taking you there because it's where I live,'' he said brusquely. ''My home is there. My office. I have people who depend on me.''

''And I,'' she said, lifting her chin, ''have nothing and no one. Is that what you're saying, *senhor?*''

''Yes. No. Damn it, Catarina—''

''It is not proper for a man to use such language in front of a woman.'' Tears burned her eyes. *You will not cry,* she told herself, and lifted her chin a notch. ''Neither is it proper for a man to address a woman so intimately.''

''Great. Just great! Is that how you're going to handle things? Each time we get to an impasse you're going to toss some ridiculous nineteenth-century rule of etiquette in my face?''

''Etiquette is the glue that holds society together.''

''Oh, for God's sake!'' Jake strode toward her, his eyes

snapping with anger. "Stop quoting Mother Elisabete to me. Maybe I haven't made this clear. You're done with that school, done with its antiquated notions. This time next week you'll be living in New York, wearing clothes that don't look as if they were sewn together by a—a band of monkeys, meeting people—"

"I made my clothes myself," she said, and the tears she'd tried to control began streaming down her cheeks.

"Catarina. I'm sorry. I didn't mean to insult you, but—"

"I hated that class," she sobbed. "I hate sewing!"

Hell, Jake thought unhappily. He put his arm around her. "Don't cry."

"I'm not crying," she said, her tears coming faster and harder. "I never cry."

Maybe not, but right now she was weeping as if her heart were going to break. Clumsily, Jake drew her closer, put his other arm around her and patted her on the back.

"And I won't be meeting people. I'll be meeting men so you can find me a proper Brazilian husband. Do you know what that means, *senhor*?"

Jake didn't know what anything meant. Not with Catarina in his arms. He'd meant his gesture to be kind. Brotherly. Avuncular. Yet somehow she was pressed against him, her body warm and supple against his.

Her face was buried against his shoulder; her hair brushed his nose. She smelled of soap and shampoo and sorrow, and he was the cause of it. Her unhappiness was all his fault.

"A proper Brazilian husband," she sobbed, "will be a man who believes he owns me."

"Hush," Jake said softly, sweeping his hand up, then down her spine.

"That's how it is here. Men are kings!"

"I won't choose someone like that."

"You'll choose the first man who meets the criteria of the will!" She drew back in his arms and stared up at him through tear-washed eyes. "You said it yourself. You have only two months to marry me off."

"Catarina—"

"I don't understand how you can do this! What can you possibly gain that's so important?"

Jake had no answer. What could he say that wouldn't reveal more about himself than he'd ever revealed to another person? Could he say *I have two half-brothers somewhere in this world but I don't know who they are?* Could he admit he'd been sired by a man who had the morals of a tomcat?

And why should he have to explain himself to this woman? No matter how you looked at it, none of this was his doing.

Jake took a deep breath, let go of her and stepped back.

"It's late," he said flatly, "and we have a long day tomorrow."

Her eyes, still bright with tears, now also glittered with defiance.

"I'm not going with you, *senhor.*"

"You most certainly are. And, though I'm sure you can quote me something appropriately pithy about the benefits of formal address, I'm tired of hearing you call me *senhor* and even more tired of hearing the twist you put on the word. My name is Jake."

"Mother Elisabete said it was Joaquim."

"It's Jake," he said sharply. "And that's how you'll address me."

"Fine. I don't care one way or the other."

The message was clear. She didn't care because she had no intention of letting him take her north.

Jake swung away, ran his hands through his hair and paced across the room. How did a man keep a woman from running off? Someday, when this nightmare was over, he was pretty sure he'd look back and laugh at the question.

He'd never had to worry about a woman running away from him.

Until tonight.

There was no lock on the outside of either bedroom door. What could he do? Put her in her room, shut the door, lie down in front of it and block it with his body? Sleeping on the floor wasn't a problem. He was tired enough to sleep on a bed of nails. And that *was* the problem. Once he fell asleep, a herd of elephants could probably tiptoe over him and he'd never stir.

He could think of only one method, but before he resorted to it he'd be a gentleman and give Catarina the chance to be a lady.

"They seem to have taught you a lot of things in that convent," he said. "Did they also teach you the importance of honor?"

Catarina, standing a few feet away, dry-eyed now, but with her arms folded and a look on her face that suggested she was trapped in a small place with a monster, raised her eyebrows.

"Of course," she said. "Honor is everything."

"And giving your word to someone? Is that a matter of honor?"

She was wary now; he could see it in the sudden tilt of her head. "Certainly."

Jake nodded. "I'm happy to hear it, because I'm asking you to give me your word that you won't try and sneak out of this room tonight."

"Fine. I give you my word that I won't try and sneak out of this room tonight."

"In that case, I'm going to bed. So are you. And you're going to remember that giving your word is a matter of—" Jake narrowed his eyes. He'd almost tumbled into her trap.

Catarina squealed as he clamped his hand around her wrist.

"What are you doing?"

A stupid question. What he was doing was dragging her to his bedroom.

"Stop it! *Senhor!*" She dug in her heels, grabbed the doorjamb. "Jake! You cannot—"

"You're good," he said, "damned good." Her hand slid from the jamb as he tugged her into his room and elbowed the door closed. "But not quite good enough."

"You asked me to give you my word I wouldn't try and escape, and I did!"

Still hanging on to her, Jake marched to the luggage rack, opened the suitcase he'd never unpacked, rummaged through it and took out a silk tie. "Sit down."

"No! Are you crazy?"

He put a hand in the middle of her chest and shoved. Catarina fell back against the bed pillows, eyes wild, breasts heaving.

"'I give you my word,'" he mimicked, his voice a high-pitched mockery of hers, "'that I won't try and sneak out of this room tonight.' *Try,*" he repeated coldly, putting emphasis on the word. "That's what you vowed, that you wouldn't *try* to escape, not that you wouldn't do it."

Her heart hammered in her ears. "I'll scream. So help me, I'll bring everyone in this hotel running!"

"You do that. By now half the staff are probably in the hall, just waiting to hear you go nuts so they can watch the men in white coats come and take you away."

He reached for her. She slapped at his hand. He cursed, grabbed her anyway, wrapped the silk tie around her wrist, wrapped it around his and made the kind of knot a Boy Scout would have admired. She was still sputtering when he pushed her back on the bed and lay down beside her.

"You can't do this!"

"Shut up."

"I will not! I am not going to sleep with—"

She gasped as he leaned over her. His eyes had gone from green to black. "You're right. You're not going to sleep with me. You're going to sleep next to me."

"Words," she said, and tried to figure out why his mocking laugh changed her fear to anger, why his closeness was changing her anger to something else.

"Trust me, kid. There's a big difference between sleeping *with* a man and sleeping *next* to him."

"I am not a kid."

"What you are," Jake said, "is a pain in the—"

To hell with it.

He reached past her, shut off the bedside light and lay back against the pillows.

"I hate you!"

"Yeah. You already told me that."

"I despise you!"

Jake yawned. "Sticks and stones," he said, and then he was silent.

He was asleep.

Catarina lay staring at the shadowy ceiling. This couldn't be happening. She was in a man's bed. She was sleeping with a man and, yes, she knew what that meant. Knew what the books said that meant, anyway. What a couple of the girls had said that meant, when they returned from weekends home.

Images danced in her mind. Heat rose in her face. She would not think of such things. They were sinful. Besides, she hated Jake Ramirez. Hated, hated, hated him!

He was the enemy.

He was also the unknown.

Catarina swallowed dryly.

If she moved, even a little, her body would brush Jake's. Not that she wanted that to happen, but if it did...if it did, so what? He was asleep. He was harmless.

And if she touched him she might learn things that would

e helpful. Things she should learn about men. She knew,
f course, about the basic male-female anatomical differ-
nces. She was naïve, but that didn't mean she was stupid.

But there were other things—things she didn't know.

Jake's body didn't just look different than hers, it felt
ifferent. When she'd slugged him, when he'd dragged her
n here with him... He was all hard muscle. Was that be-
ause he'd been tense and angry? Or would he feel that way
f she touched him when he was relaxed, too?

Hadn't some historian said you had to know the enemy
o conquer him?

Slowly, carefully, Catarina turned onto her side. Edged
p on her elbow. Looked down at the man lying beside her.

"*Senhor?*" she whispered. "Jake?"

He didn't answer. Didn't move. The slow rise and fall of
is chest assured her that he really was asleep.

He was a beautiful man.

Was that a strange word to use? Perhaps, but no other
vord fit. Jake was gorgeous. Dark, thick hair. Long, sooty
ashes. She knew girls who'd cheerfully kill for lashes like
hat. A straight nose, that full, lush mouth and strong chin...

Michelangelo couldn't have done better.

Catarina leaned closer. Inhaled. Drew in the combined
cents of soap, water and man. It was sexy. Incredibly
exy...and it was time to move away. Lie back on her side
f the bed. Try and get some sleep.

But first, first...

She caught her lip between her teeth. Lowered her hand
ntil it hovered above Jake's chest. Lowered it again until
er palm just brushed his shirt. The shirt was cotton. Thin.
'he fabric was almost transparent. She could see the outline
f his pectoral muscles, his ridged abdomen.

She didn't need to touch him after all. The shirt gave her
ll the answers she needed.

She touched him anyway. Laid her palm flat against his

chest. Felt the heat of him, the strength, the strong beat of his heart.

Her heart was beating hard, too. It was racing. She leaned closer. Closer still. Until her lips were a whisper from Jake's. Closed her eyes, traced the outline of that hard, masculine mouth with the tip of her finger. Left her finger there, lying lightly across his lips.

His beautiful lips.

What if he woke? Found her doing this? It could be dangerous. He could lose control. Men did, didn't they? The sisters had said so.

He might grasp her shoulders, roll her beneath him. Tear open her nightgown, clasp her wrists high above her head, hold her captive while he kissed her. Rubbed that sexy stubble on his jaw lightly against her throat.

Her breasts.

Her nipples.

Her nipples, tightening even as she closed her eyes and imagined it happening. *God. Oh, God. Oh…*

Jake's mouth twitched under her hand. Heart pounding, Catarina pulled away, as far as the length of silk would permit. She fell back against the pillows and lay still.

Was he awake?

He didn't move. Neither did she. After a minute, after an eternity, she turned her head and stared at him.

He was still asleep.

She let out a long, shaky breath. What had possessed her? Had she lost her mind?

She was tired. That was what it was. She was exhausted. That was the only reason she wanted—she wanted—

Catarina squeezed her eyes shut. And tumbled into a deep, dreamless sleep.

CHAPTER FIVE

How long could a man pretend to be asleep before he lost his mind?

Jake forced himself to lie still until Catarina's slow, soft breathing told him she was sleeping. Then he untied their wrists, rolled off the bed and damned near staggered out the door.

Was she crazy?

Being naïve was one thing, but a woman who bent over a sleeping man so that her hair fell around him like a silk curtain, who came so near that he could draw the feminine scent of her deep into his lungs, wasn't naïve, she was out of her mind.

Jake groaned, sank down in a chair and buried his head in his hands.

She'd touched his face. His chest. He'd figured his heart would leap out right then, but he'd hung on until she began tracing his mouth with her finger, and he'd imagined what it would be like to part his lips, draw that finger into his mouth...

He sat up and stared blindly at the sitting room wall.

Someday he'd have to look up the guy who'd given him and his roommates a quick course in meditation his first year at college.

Hey, Bill, he'd say, *thanks for saving my butt one night in Rio.*

And to think he'd almost laughed aside the offer, then fallen in with everybody else because the guy had sworn it was the reason he'd scored a bunch of As first semester.

Jake had come up with a mixed bag of grades, but tonight—tonight, without those half-forgotten mental exercises, his pulse-rate would have quadrupled and he'd have come off the bed at the speed of sound, tumbled Catarina beneath him, stripped off her clothes and buried himself deep inside her.

And that would only have been the start.

Jake shot to his feet, went to the minibar, took out a doll-sized bottle of brandy and drank down the contents.

He was in trouble. Deep trouble. His only out was to get back to New York, find a husband for Catarina as fast as he could, then wave goodbye as she turned into another man's problem.

Another man's pleasure.

A muscle knotted in his jaw.

"Damn you, Enrique," Jake muttered. He went back to the minibar, took out another toy bottle of brandy and drained it dry.

Then he lay down on a sofa that was too short, too narrow, too much like the rack in a dungeon he deserved, and did his best to get some sleep.

Catarina awakened to the sound of rain.

Remarkable, she thought drowsily, that it would rain in Rio this time of year.

Her eyes flew open. But not half as remarkable as the fact that she'd spent the night in bed with a man.

She shot up against the pillows before she realized she was alone. No Jake, just an empty space beside her. The only reminder of the night was the brightly colored length of silk he'd used to bind her to him. It lay draped over the headboard like an exotic snake.

That…and the memory of how she'd touched him while he slept. But why waste time thinking about those moments? A little temporary insanity after the day she'd endured was understandable.

What she *did* have to think about was escape. Jake could not take her to the States. She would not permit it.

Where was he, anyway? Probably on the other side of the closed door, waiting for her in the sitting room.

Her dress and leather satchel were on a chair. Courtesy of her captor, no doubt. Catarina grabbed both, went into the bathroom, locked the door and got fresh undergarments and her toothbrush from the satchel.

Moments later, she stepped back into the room.

She was still alone, but she knew better than to hope that Jake was gone. She knew precious little about him, but she'd have bet her life he wasn't a man to walk away from something he saw as his responsibility—though how she'd become that was beyond her.

Okay. Catarina took a deep breath. He was waiting in the next room—unless she'd gotten lucky. Maybe he was in the second bedroom. Maybe he'd stepped out. Gone down for breakfast, to get a newspaper, to do whatever a man like him did in the morning.

Maybe now was her chance to get away.

If she could slip out of the suite, make it to the lobby, then to the front doors… Yes, but how? Jake had spread a story that she was a crazy woman. A quick look in the mirror assured her that his story was believable.

She was an unholy mess.

She wouldn't have thought her dress, which was functional if not pretty, could look any worse than the day she'd put in the final stitches. It did. The dress was a mass of wrinkles.

And her hair looked like a demented bird's idea of a nest. She was an awful sight. Compared to the women Jake Ramirez normally slept with, she was probably…

Heat rose in her face.

She hadn't slept *with* him, she'd slept *beside* him. Anyway, why did she give a damn about the women he knew? They probably fought over the right to get his attention. Well, she had his attention and she wished to heaven she didn't—and if she stood around here much longer she'd be the victim of his attention all over again.

Her shoes were beside the bed. Better not to put them on. She could tiptoe past the other bedroom, assuming Jake was in it. Catarina scooped up the shoes, pressed her ear to the door and listened. Not a sound. Nothing but the swoosh swoosh of her pulse. Slowly she closed her hand around the knob, turned it, held her breath as she swung the door open…

And saw Jake, sitting in an armchair, watching her. He had an open newspaper in his lap, a steaming cup of coffee next to him, and a polite smile on his face.

"Good morning." His gaze traveled to the shoes hanging from her fingers. "Going somewhere?"

She was disappointed, but not intimidated. There'd always been someone watching you at school; if you got caught doing what you weren't supposed to do, you simply lied your way out of it. With a white lie, of course. White lies were not only acceptable, they were necessities when you lived inside the gates of the convent…

When a man appeared out of the blue and tried to ruin your life.

"Yes," she said, her smile as polite as his. "I wanted to get my toothbrush. I left it in the other bathroom."

"And you're walking barefoot so as not to disturb me? How thoughtful… Or do you always travel on tiptoe?"

She felt her face heat but she kept her eyes steady on his. "I don't know what you mean."

Jake nodded at the shoes in her hand. "Perhaps the custom here is different. Back in the States, shoes are generally worn on the feet, not the hands."

"My feet hurt."

"Of course." Another polite smile. "Well, you can put

on a pair of more comfortable shoes after you brush your teeth.''

''Oh. Yes, of course. I—I—''

''Would you like some coffee? There's a second cup.''

She would, desperately, but accepting anything from him would be a sign of defeat.

''No,'' she said, and then, though it killed her, she added, ''Thank you.''

Jake folded the paper. ''I was just about to wake you.''

An image of herself in bed flashed before her, Jake bending over her, softly saying her name, reaching down to cup her face and lift it to his...

How long did temporary insanity last?

''How nice for us both that it wasn't necessary,'' she said, marching past him to the bedroom.

Catarina slammed the door after her, hard enough to rattle Jake's teeth. Great, he thought, tossing the paper aside. Just great. Another day, another confrontation. What else was new?

What had happened last night. That was new.

Lying there when she'd decided to go on her little journey of discovery. Not moving a muscle when she bent over him, touched him...

Even remembering made him hard as stone, but there was no point to it.

He'd find someone who'd be right for Catarina. A good guy. A young one—she deserved that. Somebody she'd want to be with. Somebody who'd teach her the endless things she didn't know about men and life and sex...

The things he'd ached to teach her last night.

''Damn it all,'' Jake snarled, and stalked across the room. ''Catarina!'' He slammed his fist against the bedroom door and bellowed her name again. ''Catarina! Get a move on!''

He'd already jammed the inside lock. The hotel could bill him for it. They could bill him for the whole door if he got any angrier and kicked it down. Where was she? What took so long? They were on the top floor, but for all he knew she was crazy enough—desperate enough—to try and jimmy open the win—

The door swung open.

"There's no need to make so much noise."

She sounded calm, but he saw that she hadn't put on her shoes.

"You're not ready."

Catarina's face was a blank. "Ready for what?"

"Look, it's barely seven in the morning. That makes it a little early for riddles. Maybe things start early in your school, but—"

"It isn't my school. Actually, it hasn't been for a long time. I should have left there three years ago."

Jake dug his hands into his trouser pockets and rocked back a little on his heels.

"Strange. I could have sworn I collected you there just yesterday."

"You 'collected' me," she said, "because my guardian wouldn't let me leave."

"You've got that wrong. It was your parents' will that wouldn't let you leave."

"Put it any way you like. I was kept there, enrolled in useless courses—"

"Sewing," he said, with a little smile.

An arrogant smile, but she wasn't going to let him rattle her. She'd considered her options carefully and reached a simple conclusion. If you behaved like a supplicant, you were treated like one. The only chance she had of getting Jake Ramirez to listen to reason was to stop pleading for understanding and start demanding it.

"The point is," she said calmly, "those days are over."

"The days you studied sewing?"

"Do you think this is a joke, Mr. Ramirez? I assure you, it isn't. It's deadly serious to me."

Mr. Ramirez? Jake thought. Hadn't he told her to call him Jake? Not that he gave a damn; what she called him was her business. And hell, no, this wasn't a joke. This was a bad dream and he was only trying to make the best of it.

All he wanted was her cooperation and, okay, maybe he wasn't encouraging it with this little session of give-and-take, but who was she kidding with this lady-of-the-manor routine? Was he supposed to be impressed?

The only thing that did impress him was the way she looked. Her hair, loose and wild, had seemed a disaster area last night. Now that she'd given up trying to tame it, it was...

Okay. Sexy was the wrong word. Pretty. Her hair was pretty. Yeah. That was lots better.

So were her eyes, snapping with anger. Her cheeks, flushed with color. That dress, that god-awful dress, was still ugly, still wrinkled, still the garment of a child—except now he knew it concealed the body of a woman. And what was he doing, thinking about that again?

She was a kid. An innocent. A virgin straight out of a convent school.

She was his ward. His defiant, furious, impossible ward, and, yes, all right, his gorgeous and sexy-as-hell ward, too. So what? None of that changed the fact that he was stuck with her.

No way was she going to make him out to be a monster.

"You're right," he said briskly. "This isn't funny, and it isn't a situation you can talk your way out of." He moved past her, grabbed her satchel, then picked up his case. "We have a plane to catch."

"No."

"Look at it this way. The sooner we get to New York, the sooner we can get started on ending this relationship."

"We can end it right now," Catarina said quickly. "All you have to do is—"

"You've got that wrong. All *you* have to do is behave yourself."

Catarina stared at Jake. His face was stony, his eyes cold. Whatever little game he'd been playing with her the past few minutes was over.

Panic coiled in her belly.

"Your move, kid. You gonna put on your shoes or you want to take this trip barefoot?"

"I told you, I am not a kid!"

"Fine. You're Methuselah. Just get going."

"I'll make a scene at the airport!"

"I know you're out of touch with the real world," Jake said grimly, "but you pull a stunt like that I can almost guarantee you'll end up in handcuffs."

"Not after I tell the police everything. How you're forcing me to leave the country. How you have no right to—"

Jake dropped her satchel and the suitcase. Catarina cried out as he caught her by the shoulders and lifted her to her toes.

"You don't have any rights," he said coldly, "unless I say so."

She was staring at him as if he really was a monster, but he didn't care. She didn't want to go with him? Tough. He didn't want her going with him. What she couldn't seem to grasp was that what she wanted, what he wanted, didn't matter.

He'd never believed in an afterlife, but he was sure as hell starting to change his mind. Why else would her parents and his son of a bitch of a father have put them into this situation if they weren't sitting on a fluffy cloud, laughing themselves sick over what they'd accomplished?

And now, damn it, she was starting to cry. Big, perfect,

tears were streaming down her cheeks. This time he wasn't going to let them affect him.

"Stop that," he said gruffly.

"How can you do this? I'm not a—a package you can transport and dispose of."

"FedEx deals with packages," he said, in a desperate attempt at humor. "We'll be flying first class."

She gave him exactly the sort of look a remark that pitiful deserved. Maybe it was time to try a different approach.

"Deal with what's happened, Catarina, and move on."

"Oh, that sounds so brave. Deal with it. Move on. Except you aren't the one whose life is being turned upside down."

Jake picked up the bags so one was under his arm. "It damned well is," he said, grabbing her elbow, "and I've had it with this discussion." He felt her start to pull away and slid his hand to her wrist. "The sooner you accept that we're stuck with each other, the better."

Her eyes met his. All the bluff was gone, the pride that had protected her from accepting her fate. She looked terrified.

And he felt like the biggest son of a bitch in the universe.

He told himself he didn't have to do this. He could say to hell with Enrique, to hell with everything and walk away—or he could take this woman in his arms, rock her against him until her panic faded while he told her that everything would be okay.

Except it would be a lie.

Things weren't going to be okay. Not for her, not for him. Not until they'd both finished dancing to the tune played by a trio of cosmic jokesters—and even then there'd be no guarantees.

"Did you hear me?" he said sharply. "No more tears. I'm tired of the-routine."

"I hate you," she whispered.

"That's a kid's response." He wanted to sound angry but

he had the feeling he wasn't quite pulling it off. Maybe it was because he could see the fight going out of her, see resignation dulling her lovely eyes.

"I hate you, hate you, hate—"

Catarina cried out as Jake dropped the bags again, hauled her to her toes, pulled her against him and crushed her mouth under his.

He kissed her unmercifully, with an adult passion he knew would only add to her terror. It was deliberate. Let her see what it meant to be a woman instead of a child...

And then he stopped thinking.

He felt the shudder that ran through her, heard her smothered cry, tasted the salt of her tears and he groaned, slid his hands into her hair and kissed her as if this were not just her first kiss but his.

He kissed her tenderly. Softly. Kissed her and kissed her until her trembling stopped, until her lips softened. Until she sighed and opened her mouth to his and he tasted her sweetness.

Her innocence.

Let go of her, he told himself. *Damn it, Ramirez, let go.*

But he didn't. Instead he drew her closer. Catarina raised her arms, wrapped them around his neck, leaned into him and whispered something against his mouth, something his brain couldn't understand but his body—God, his body understood it completely.

Jake forgot her innocence.

Forgot everything but the feel of her in his arms.

"Cat," he murmured. "Cat." And he ran his hands down her back, cupped her buttocks, lifted her to him, moved against her, let her feel how much he wanted her, how powerful his desire was, and...

And what in hell was he doing?

He jerked back. Let go of Catarina. Stared down at her

face, still raised to his, saw her parted lips, the pulse beating in her throat, the dark curve of her lashes against her cheeks.

Then she opened her eyes and he knew that her stunned expression would haunt him long after fate finally let them go their separate ways.

''You see?'' he said calmly, as if his ears weren't filled with the thundering beat of his own heart. ''You're a child after all.''

He opened the door, picked up the luggage once more and stepped into the corridor. He didn't look back. He didn't have to. The kiss had changed the rules of the game. If her stubborn pride had been important to Catarina before, it had to be the only thing she could cling to now.

He was counting on it to make her follow him.

Damned if he wasn't right.

CHAPTER SIX

GETTING tough worked.

Or maybe it was the kiss.

That was why he'd kissed her, after all. Why he'd turned the kiss into something she'd remember. Just to rattle Catarina's cage. Make her see he was serious.

There wasn't any other reason.

When the elevator doors opened on the lobby, Jake headed straight for the exit. No backward glances, no clamping his hand around Cat's wrist and hauling her alongside him.

He acted as if he were sure she'd follow him.

The truth was, he was sure of absolutely nothing.

Would she bolt and run? Would she start screaming? Would he end up explaining how he'd gotten into this mess to the local cops as well as to the guys in white coats?

The prospect was not appealing. Explaining that a full-grown woman was, in all ways that mattered, his legal ward wasn't something he looked forward to, but if he had to do it he would.

The skin on the back of his neck prickled as he strode out the door. Was she still following him? Yeah. She was. He stopped short as the parking valet trotted over. Catarina barreled into him. Jake took advantage of the moment to slip an arm around her shoulders and draw her forward.

No sense in pushing his luck out here on the street.

The valet wasn't the one who'd parked Jake's rental car the prior night, but judging by the look the boy gave them word about the North American and his crazy niece must have spread.

"*Bom dia, senhor.*"

Jake smiled pleasantly. "Good morning. My car is the black—"

"*Sim.* I know. *Um momento, por favor.*"

Oh, yeah. The word had definitely spread. The kid trotted off and Jake bent his head and put his lips to Catarina's ear.

"Very good," he said quietly. "Just keep it up and we'll get along fine."

She jerked back and glared at him. "That's probably what the *bandeirantes* told the Indians."

The words might have been formed in ice. Jake didn't delude himself into thinking he'd just been given a compliment.

"Raiders," she said venomously. "Portuguese barbarians who stormed the interior of Brazil and forced the natives into slavery."

"And that's me?" He nodded. "Nice. Really nice."

"Accurate, you mean."

"I don't suppose it would do any good to point out that I'm not Portuguese and you're not Indian."

"The principle's the same." She gave him a smile that matched her tone. "I notice you didn't try and argue about what they did."

"I don't know what they did," he said politely, "aside from what you've told me. I believe your point is that I have a lot in common with a bunch of stormtroopers."

"Exactly. And I'd appreciate it if you'd take your hands off me."

Jake sighed. Yesterday had seemed endless, and if he'd had an hour of solid sleep last night it was a lot. He couldn't let Catarina bait him. He was liable to end up slinging her over his shoulder and carrying her onto the plane—or taking her in his arms and kissing her until she turned soft and sweet and clinging again.

He knew damned well that neither method was a very good idea.

The valet roared up in the car, stopped on a dime and bounded out from behind the wheel. Jake handed him a couple of bills. The kid dumped the two bags in the back, hurried around to the passenger side and yanked open the door.

Jake slid his hand to Catarina's wrist and marched her around the vehicle.

"You seem to be a smart girl," he said softly. "So here's what *I'd* appreciate. You get in the car, behave yourself, keep your mouth shut until we land in New York. Then we can have a long talk about raiders, stormtroopers and Indians. How's that sound?"

"It sounds as if I have no choice in the matter."

"A brilliant conclusion."

"Just understand that my acquiescence is based on expediency, not obedience."

Jake's eyebrows shot toward his hairline. "I'll bet you got straight As in English."

"I got straight As in everything," she said smugly. "Would you like to know what the words mean?"

"Thanks for the offer, but I can manage. You want me to know that you're going along with this because I'm bigger, stronger and nastier than you are. Right?"

Color flooded her face. "It's not that simple."

"I think it is."

"You're an awful man, Mr. Ramirez."

"'You're an awful man, *Jake,*'" he said. "Now, get in the damned car."

"There's no need for obscenities."

"You think that's an obscenity?" he said through his teeth. "Trust me, Catarina. You haven't heard anything yet. Now, move!"

She gave him a look that Medusa might have used to turn

men to stone. Except she didn't look like Medusa this morning; she looked more like a woman trying not to show the depth of her terror.

Jake sighed.

"Catarina." He hesitated. "I know this isn't easy."

"Your brilliance astounds me."

Not even her sarcasm could hide what he saw in her eyes.

"I just want you to know that I'll try my best to do the right thing for you."

Her mouth trembled. "Will you?"

He nodded. "You behave yourself and I'll—I'll make this whole thing as painless as possible. Deal?"

She stared at his outstretched hand as if it might transmit bubonic plague. Just when he thought he'd been a fool to offer a flag of truce, she put her hand in his.

For all her bravado, her skin was icy.

"Deal," she said, and Jake wondered, if only for a minute, what she'd do if he changed their handshake into a kiss.

The flight to New York seemed interminable.

Catarina didn't mind. It gave her time to think.

Did Jake mean what he said about doing the right thing? She'd seen a sudden compassion in his eyes when he'd spoken.

Maybe he wouldn't marry her off.

No. He would. But he'd try and find a decent man for her. That would be his version of "the right thing."

That meant her version of "the right thing" had to be learning all she could about men.

And sex.

Jake didn't know it—wouldn't know it—but she'd decided to go along with things. She really didn't have a choice. Her guardian wasn't going to give an inch, and escape, she had to admit, wasn't a possibility.

Catarina shot Jake a quick look. He was sitting beside

her, seat tilted, long legs outstretched. His head was back, his eyes closed, his hands loosely folded in his lap. He looked like a big, lazy cat—except she knew that was deceptive. The same as a cat, he could spring in a heartbeat.

Catarina turned her face to the window. He was right. She had to move on. Make the best of what had happened.

And that kiss had given her an idea.

She knew Jake had kissed her to show her that she was defenseless against him. That he was strong and she was weak, that he was male and she was female, and that she didn't know the first thing about how such relationships worked.

He was right on all counts, especially the last.

She didn't know the first thing about the intricate dance between men and women—not even after hushed late-night conversations in the dorm when one of the girls had returned from a weekend at home.

The topic was almost always sex.

He did what? she or one of the others would say in horror. *And you let him?*

Why would a woman let a man do…? Well, why would she?

That kiss had provided some vague idea. Once she'd let herself sink into the moment, let Jake's lips shape hers, his body heat hers, she'd had an inkling of why the girl telling the story would laugh and say, yes, of course she'd let the boy do this and that and the other thing.

Sex was incredibly powerful.

It was pathetic to first learn such a lesson when you were twenty-one, but at least she'd learned it before her guardian married her off. Marriage was no place for on-the-job training—especially since the odds were excellent that her husband would be the suitable Brazilian as demanded by the terms of her parents' will.

Jake would find her a rich man who'd take over the handling of both her money and her life. He'd expect her to know her place. Almost without question, he'd be older.

And he'd want to do things to her in bed.

She couldn't go into such a marriage blind. Until yesterday she'd known nothing about men. Literally nothing. She knew a little now, all of it picked up in—Catarina frowned and checked her watch—in the past twenty-four hours.

She had Jake to thank.

Because of him she knew that that men had tempers. That they were intractable. That they'd agree to do outlandish things as long as they could convince themselves they did them to live up to some sacred code of honor.

Catarina ran the tip of her tongue across her lips.

She knew, as well, that the thing she knew the least about—the physical thing, sex—was more complex than she'd anticipated.

Just look at those wild ideas she'd had last night, when she was in bed with Jake. She'd shocked herself. No. Wrong. She'd frightened herself. The same as he had frightened her when he'd kissed her this morning.

That was what sex was all about. Power.

It was, wasn't it?

Then how come her bones had all but turned liquid when she'd imagined him making love to her? How come even when he'd been kissing her, when his kiss had been harsh and demanding to show her he could control her, she'd liked it?

She drew a shaky breath.

Even then she'd liked it.

In a heartbeat she'd gone from feeling small and helpless to delicate and eager. Jake's size, the way he'd held her so she couldn't escape him, the way he'd tilted her head back as if to emphasize the difference between his strength and her fragility, had stirred her.

And then, just when she'd been about to sigh and let

herself feel what he was doing instead of analyzing it, he'd taken the kiss one hundred and eighty degrees, softened the pressure of his mouth, eased his touch, and she'd gone into meltdown.

Physically, mentally, emotionally.

Did a man's kiss always do that to a woman? If it did—and she had no reason to think otherwise—who knew what would happen if a man really made love to her? Would she turn into an obedient slave? Weren't there ways to prevent that? Couldn't you ward off that devastating meltdown?

No way was she going to wait until she was locked in marriage to find the answers. She needed them now, long before she had to deal with the intricacies of wedlock.

Jake would teach her. She'd learn all she could from him.

Not that she'd let things go All The Way. She knew what that was, more or less. Jake had asked if they'd talked about sex in Health Class and she'd said no, they hadn't, which wasn't exactly true. Sister Angelica had mentioned the word once, said it was a Wife's Duty and crossed herself.

She'd never been more specific than that.

One of the girls had been a lot more specific, whispering things late at night that Catarina had never quite believed were physically possible.

Jake could teach her. Not everything, but enough. She would not go into marriage completely uninformed.

She glanced at him again.

Of course there were probably other factors to consider. Jake was good-looking. Very. And he was young. Being made love to by a man like him would probably be different than being made love to by one who was old or ugly—like that fat businessman across the aisle, snoring away in happy oblivion, or the attorney, Estes, with his skinny little moustache and a bunch of white hairs growing out of his ears.

Catarina shuddered.

No. She couldn't count on the man Jake chose for her

looking like him. She couldn't count on lying beside him at night and having the delicious freedom to touch him, find out where that silky arrow of hair on his flat belly went after it vanished under the waistband of his trousers...

"Flight attendants, prepare the cabin for arrival."

Catarina sat up straight.

Arrival indeed, she thought, and emptied her mind of everything but the one thing that mattered.

Survival.

Rio was big and, even on a rainy day, cheerful.

New York was grey, cold, and as cheerless as a tomb.

Maybe it was the press of traffic. The crowded sidewalks. The tall buildings leaning in. Maybe it was because every other woman she saw—make that *every* woman she saw— was dressed in black. Chic black, but black nevertheless.

Jake's apartment was on Fifth Avenue, across from a huge stretch of green.

"Central Park," he said, when she all but pasted her nose to the taxi window.

She wanted to ask him why this was called Fifth Avenue instead of Park, since Park didn't face anything close to grass and Fifth did. She wanted to ask him, too, where the *favelas* were located. Surely there were poor people living in this city.

But she didn't. It was bad enough he'd caught her gawking at the scenery. He thought she was a country mouse. A childish country mouse. Why feed into that if she could avoid it?

His apartment was in a tall building facing the park. Gargoyles peered from the cornices and looked down at the street. The doorman greeted him by name and touched his cap politely at the sight of her. The elevator starter did the same before inserting a key into a slot.

A paneled and carpeted car whisked them up to the top floor.

To the top two floors. Jake's apartment was a huge duplex with a breathtaking view. He led her down a long hall to a bedroom and connecting bath he said would be hers, and she was happy to see the rooms overlooked the park, too. The trees far below were gaunt and leafless, but she didn't mind. There was something elegant about them, like monochrome sketches that matched the gray city sky.

Catarina had never seen such luxury or even imagined it. Her parents' home had been handsome, but this was opulent. It occurred to her that she had no idea how much money it took to live this way—to live any way, for that matter—or how much she had inherited, but now wasn't the time to ask.

"I suggest you unpack," Jake said briskly, "and take a nap. Anna's not here—"

"Anna?"

He nodded. "But she knew we were coming. I phoned this morning. She'll have prepared something for dinner."

He had a wife? A mistress? And he'd kissed her? Another thing to learn about men. Though on this subject at least Catarina had already heard. Brazilian men were not known for fidelity.

Apparently, neither were Americans.

"She has no objections to me staying here?"

"Why would she?"

Why, indeed? Jake was the man. The boss. And if it troubled her at all that he belonged to another woman that was just plain stupid. It was only that if he had a wife, that would spoil her plans.

Her guardian, even the Brazilian she'd marry, might not think much of fidelity, but she did.

"No reason," Catarina said politely. "I just wasn't aware of your customs."

"My customs?"

"Your cultural customs. Regarding marriage."

He stared at her blankly. Then his mouth twitched. "You think Anna's my wife?"

"Is she your mistress?"

He came toward her slowly, his eyes locked to hers. She wanted to back up, but showing weakness would, she knew, be a mistake.

"I kissed you this morning."

Her heart thudded. "Did you?" She shrugged. "I suppose you did, but I can hardly re—"

He caught her by the shoulders, bent to her and kissed her again. Another lesson, Cat told herself, before she stopped thinking.

His mouth was warm. Soft against hers. She felt the tip of his tongue at the seam of her lips and she made an inadvertent little sound, the barest whisper, but it was all he needed to take the kiss deeper. She made the sound again, something that was part moan, part sigh, and Jake groaned, cupped her face with his hands, tilted her head back and angled his mouth over hers until she knew she'd fall if she didn't reach up, grasp his shirt, bunch it in her fists...

"Do you remember now?"

His mouth was a breath away.

"Yes," she said, and hated how shaky her voice sounded. Jake might not know it yet, but he was her teacher. That was all. She had to approach this clinically. "Yes," she said, more briskly. "I suppose I—"

Jake's mouth took hers again. He wrapped his arms around her, pulled her against him, let her feel his heat and his swift arousal. It was all to serve a purpose, he told himself. The woman had to understand she couldn't play with him unless she wanted to get burned.

But the flame was dangerous for him, too.

God, the taste of her. The feel of her. She was pressed

hard against him, her breasts soft against his chest, her hips tucked against his, but it wasn't enough.

He wanted more.

He wanted to open her dress, bare her breasts. Cup them. Caress them. Skim his fingers over her nipples and watch her face when he did. Hear her cry out his name as he tore the dress from her shoulders, slid his hand into her panties, found that hot, sweet heart of her femininity that wept softly for him, only for him.

Take her innocence. Her perfect innocence.

Innocence she would bring to another man.

Jake tore his mouth from Cat's. She swayed in his arms. "Jake?" she whispered, and he let go of her, knotted his hands into fists before he could reach for her again, and dug them into his pockets.

"How about now?" he said, so calmly that he wanted to applaud his performance. "Your memory any better?"

Cat's eyes opened. She blinked and he wondered if he'd ever seen lashes as long as hers before. Then she touched the tip of her pale pink tongue to her bottom lip, and his libido threatened to wipe out his brain.

"I asked you a question," he said gruffly. "Has your memory improved?"

Her head dipped in jerky assent. "Yes."

"Good."

She did it again, that little thing with her tongue. Jake took a quick step back.

"I wouldn't have kissed you if I had a wife. Or a mistress."

"Why not? In Brazil—"

"Yeah. In my country, too, sometimes. Maybe it's an old-fashioned concept, but I'm into commitment. I mean," he said hastily, "I'm not actually *into* it. Not yet. But when and if I find the right woman I won't fool around with anybody else."

"Is that what you're doing with me? Fooling around?"

Hell. How did he manage to dig himself deeper with every word?

"I'm talking about kissing you. I wouldn't have done it if there was anyone else."

Really? What about Samantha Vickers? And how come he hadn't thought of Sam once since he'd gone to that convent?

"So you kissed me because you're not committed to anyone?"

"Yes. No." He ran his hand through his hair. Two months of this, he'd be a basket-case. "I kissed you, that's all. A kiss is just a kiss. It isn't always an earth-shaking event."

"Some of the girls said it was. And some of the books I read…"

Catarina looked down. Jake put his hand under her chin and lifted her face until their eyes met.

"Some of what books?"

"Never mind."

"Come on, Cat. What books?"

She turned a pale pink. "The girls who went home for weekends, you know, sometimes they brought back books."

Lady Chatterley's Lover? The Story of O? Jake narrowed his eyes. "And?"

"And in those books…"

"What books, damn it?"

"Romance novels. In some of them kisses were—they were special."

"Ah. Romance novels." He let out a sigh of relief. How revealing could a romance novel be? "Yeah, well, they can be."

"But they don't have to be? You mean a man can kiss a woman for no reason?"

"No. Of course not. A man should always—he should always feel—he should want the woman to feel…"

"Yes?" Cat said softly. "Feel what?"

Years before, when he was just a kid, Jake and his pals had cut school on a bitterly cold winter day. They'd gone to one of the old factory piers on the Bronx River where they swam during the summer. There'd been ice on the river and he'd walked out on its frozen skin.

"*Go, Jake!*" the other kids had yelled.

And he'd gone. Five feet from shore. Ten feet. Before he'd suddenly felt the first delicate shiver of the ice under his feet.

Suddenly the cries had been filled with terror.

"*It's breaking up, man,*" one of the kids had shouted. "*Jake, Jake, the ice is breaking. Turn around. Head back!*"

He had, because doing anything else would have been insane.

Still, there'd been that one mercurial instant when he'd hesitated, torn between the gut-loosening terror of knowing he was in danger and the indescribable high that came of flirting with it.

That was how he felt now, looking down into Catarina Mendes's coffee-colored eyes. How he felt as he watched the tip of her pink tongue dart out and slick over her bottom lip.

One step forward. One touch. One more kiss…

"Jake?"

He dragged air into his lungs, then took a step back, away from her, away from the ice that threatened to buckle under his feet.

"Unpack," he said in a low growl. "Change that damned brown sack for something else. Take a nap or pace back and forth. Either is fine with me. I'll call you when supper's ready." He stepped out of the room, began to shut the door, then remembered what had started this scene. "You asked me about Anna."

"Yes?"

"She's my housekeeper. Married. Her age is someplace between fifty and infinity."

"Oh."

"Yeah. 'Oh.' Not that it's any of your business."

"I just thought—"

"I know what you thought," Jake said, and yanked the door shut after him.

Except he really didn't. Certainly not. Because the idea that his innocent ward, his convent-bred child-woman, had been baiting him, was impossible.

She couldn't have been teasing him. Winding him up in hopes he'd kiss her again.

No way. The very idea was crazy. She couldn't. She wouldn't.

Or would she?

Jake swore, ripped off his tie, headed for the master suite at the other end of the duplex and the benefits of a long, icy shower.

CHAPTER SEVEN

IT TURNED out that Anna had left a casserole alongside a bowl of rice in the fridge: strips of chicken, mushrooms and peapods in some kind of rich brown sauce.

Five minutes in the microwave for the casserole, her accompanying note said, three minutes for the rice.

When the meal was ready, Jake went to the foot of the wide staircase that led to the upper level of the penthouse.

"Dinner's ready," he called.

No answer.

"Catarina? Supper's on."

He heard her door open. "I'm not hungry."

"Fine. Excellent. That means there's more for me."

He stomped back to the kitchen, burned his fingers taking the dishes from the nuker and put them on the breakfast bar. He was angry, angrier than he should have been at Cat's assumption that he was married or at least involved with a woman.

She had one lousy attitude about men, he thought grimly, yanking open the silverware drawer. Maybe the men she knew would fool around with one woman while they were involved with another, but—

But what?

His ward didn't know any men. She didn't know the first thing about them or how they behaved. And that was the problem, wasn't it? He was responsible for finding a husband for a woman who might as well have spent her life on one of the outer moons of the planet Zongo.

"Hell," he muttered, and plucked a fork from the drawer. He glanced at the cupboard, gave a second's consideration

90

to taking down a plate, even adding a serving spoon and napkin to the counter—but why bother? He was a bachelor, having a meal alone, thanks to the unreasonably touchy temperament of his house guest.

He was also hungry as a bear. A bear in an extremely foul mood. Add it up, and he couldn't see any reason not to pull up a stool, poke his fork into the casserole and—

"Don't you know how to set a table?"

Jake smothered a groan and let his fork clatter to the granite countertop.

"I thought you weren't hungry."

"I changed my mind." Cat gave a delicate sniff. "That smells...not too bad."

"Anna would be thrilled at that wild vote of approval."

Footsteps padded across the tile behind him. "What is it?"

"Something with chicken."

"Yes, but what? It's definitely not the awful stuff we got at school."

"Then why not call it that?" Jake said sarcastically as he turned to face her. "You know. Not The Awful Stuff We—" His jaw dropped. "A better question is, what is *that?*"

Cat glanced down at herself. She was wearing sweats. Well, that was what she called them. The truth was, the pants and shirt hadn't come out quite as intended—partly because she'd cut and sewn them on the sly, and partly because sewing, as she'd already admitted, was not her strongest skill.

"It's a sweatsuit," she said, with a lift of the chin that warned Jake to leave the topic alone. "Not up to New York standards, perhaps, but I like it."

Jake stared at her for a long minute. She'd showered. Her damp and glossy curls hung loose around her face, emphasizing its oval delicacy. The sweats were a bad joke and hung on her with room to spare. Still, he could see the thrust of her breasts beneath the cotton fabric, the roundness of her hips, the long length of her legs. Those bare toes that had turned him on before peeped out beneath the badly turned cuffs.

He wanted to laugh at the picture she made but he couldn't. Not when she also looked so sweet and vulnerable.

And incredibly, astoundingly sexy.

He swung away, rose from the stool and went to the cupboard. He took out dishes and napkins, rummaged in the drawer for forks and knives and spoons.

"Here," he said brusquely, thrusting the stuff at Catarina. "Set the table."

"Do you mean, set the counter?"

"Yes. Right. That's what I meant."

"Because there's a difference, you know, between the proper way to set a breakfast bar and a table. For the one, these paper napkins are fine, but for the other—"

"Just set the damned thing," Jake said through his teeth. "You don't have to use—"

"Obscenities. You're wrong. I do. And if you don't stop correcting me you'll hear some that'll singe your ears."

Catarina lifted her eyebrows but kept silent as she laid out the china, flatware and napkins. She needed to get her guardian in a better mood. Babbling silly lessons learned at school wasn't the way to do it, but she was nervous.

Yesterday she'd spent her first night ever in a hotel. Now she was about to spend her first night in a man's apartment.

And to present that man with a plan.

She had to find a way to take back control of her life.

Take it back? She'd never had control in the first place. The school, the sisters, Mother Elisabete, her uncle and his attorney and now Jake Ramirez... They ruled her existence.

Now she was supposed to let that long line of regulators hand her off to a man who'd rule her, too?

Not without a fight.

The first glimmer of hope had come to her as she'd showered, washing her hair with a shampoo she'd found in the guest bathroom that smelled like vanilla and felt like silk. By the time she'd moved on to drying off, she'd had the start of a plan.

She'd opened bottles and tubes, taken deep sniffs, selected one that reminded her of roses. And, as she'd rubbed it into her skin, she had suddenly known exactly how to gain her freedom.

Actually, Jake was responsible—first talking about the differences between his culture and that of Brazil...

Then taking her in his arms and kissing her.

Those kisses had—they'd aroused her. But they'd aroused him, too. She'd felt his—felt his erection press against her belly.

Catarina swallowed dryly.

Sex was potent stuff.

And that was why her scheme would work. She was sure of it. All she had to do now was find a subtle way to present it to Jake, and an even more subtle way to sell it to him.

She watched as he dumped a huge mound of the chicken casserole on her plate. What was that old saying? The way to a man's heart was through his stomach?

"That looks wonderful," she said brightly.

Jake grunted and eased onto a stool.

"How about some biscuits?"

He looked at her. "Biscuits?"

"Or muffins. Did Anne leave some?"

"Anna. And, no, she didn't."

"Too bad. If you want to wait half an hour or so, I can whip up a batch."

His gaze flattened as he looked her over from head to toe. "Are you as good a cook as you are a seamstress?"

Catarina's chin came up. "I'm an excellent cook."

"Yeah, well, I'll pass. But bread's not a bad idea. There should be some in that drawer."

She found the bread, found a small silver basket, lined it with a napkin and arranged a display of neatly overlapping slices.

"There," she said briskly. "How's that?"

"Wonderful. Now can I eat?"

"Do you want butter?"

"What I want," Jake said, "is a little peace and quiet."

"Of course." She spoke pleasantly, even though she wanted to dump the casserole over his head. She climbed onto the stool next to his, forked up some of the chicken and put it in her mouth. "Mmm. Delicious. I wonder, do you have any wine? A Château D'Este Zinfandel would—"

"Catarina."

"Yes?"

"Shut up."

So much for getting to his heart through his stomach—but then she didn't have to get to his heart, she had only to get to his brain. And, for all Jake's surliness, she had to admit he did seem to have a brain.

"Jake?"

"Yes?"

"Jake." She took a deep breath. "I've been thinking."

"In your case, always a dangerous activity."

She decided to ignore the taunt. "You're not exactly thrilled to have me as a responsibility." He didn't answer. Well, she hadn't expected him to correct her. Still, it wouldn't have killed him to be polite. "And I," she added, "am not exactly thrilled to find myself your ward."

"Amazing. We have something in common after all."

"So, as I said, I've been thinking."

Jake looked at her. "There's no way out of this," he said quietly. "None at all. You need a husband. I need to find you one. And we have precious little time in which to do it."

She nodded. "I know. But remember what you said before? About our cultures being different?"

"Did I say that?"

"Yes. We were talking about Brazilian men and American men. I said Brazilian men cheated on their wives, and you said—"

"I said a lot of things. Then I kissed you."

Silence filled the room. Their eyes met. "Yes," Cat said, after a while, "you did."

"That's not going to happen anymore."

She stared at him. "Why not?"

"Because..." Jake looked deep into those questioning eyes and understood the reason for his anger. "Because," he said gently, "it's wrong. I'm your guardian. My job is to look out for your welfare."

"Surely it doesn't hurt my welfare if you kiss me?"

Was she that naïve? Or was she playing a game? His gaze dropped to her mouth, so pink and soft and sweet. Naïve or not, he had to be more careful in his dealings with her.

"Your future husband wouldn't like it."

Her mouth trembled. "I don't even know who he is."

"Well, we're going to solve that problem ASAP."

"ASAP? What does that mean?"

"It means I'm going to make some phone calls tomorrow and get the ball rolling." Jake reached for her hand. "Cat. I'm going to find you a husband, and I'll do my best to make sure he's a good choice."

She nodded and bent her head. Her hair tumbled forward, hiding her face, and he fought back the almost overwhelming desire to touch his hand to the soft, gold-burnished curls.

"I know it isn't what you want, but—"

"But it has to be done."

"Yes. As soon as you accept that—"

"I have accepted it," she said, and looked up at him. "Fully."

Jake blinked. "What?"

"I said, I've accepted what must happen. There's no getting away from the terms of the will."

"Well," he said. "Well, I'm glad to hear… I mean, I'm glad you've finally…"

What in hell was wrong with him? How come he couldn't finish a simple sentence? Of course he was glad to hear she'd finally come to her senses. He had to marry her off. She'd accepted it. There wasn't a reason in the world her admission should bother him.

"I'm delighted you've come around," he said briskly.

"There are just a couple of conditions."

Conditions? Jake considered pointing out that she wasn't in any position to set conditions, but what harm could there be in letting her talk? What counted was that she'd agreed to stop fighting him. How impossible could her conditions be?

"What conditions?"

Cat drew her hand from his and cleared her throat. She looked like a woman preparing for a speech.

"First, a question. What does the will say about me staying married? I mean, for instance, suppose I married someone and he died? Wouldn't I have fulfilled the terms of the will? Wouldn't I be entitled to claim my inheritance?"

He looked at her in disbelief. "For God's sake, Catarina, you can't be serious! Do you really think I'd let you plan a murder?"

"Plan a…?" Cat laughed. "I'm not talking about killing anyone! I just wanted your opinion on what would happen if my marriage didn't last. I didn't want to use the D word until I knew what that opinion would be."

THE EDITOR'S "THANK YOU" FREE GIFTS INCLUDE:

▶ Two BRAND-NEW Harlequin® Next™ Novels

▶ An exciting surprise gift

YES! I have placed my Editor's "thank you" Free Gifts seal in the space provided at right. Please send me 2 FREE books, and my FREE Mystery Gift. I understand that I am under no obligation to purchase anything further, as explained on the back and opposite page.

PLACE
FREE GIFTS
SEAL
HERE

▶ DETACH AND MAIL CARD TODAY! ▶

356 HDL D74J

156 HDL D72U

FIRST NAME	LAST NAME

ADDRESS

APT.#	CITY

STATE/PROV.	ZIP/POSTAL CODE

Thank You!

(HN-PAS-11/05)

The Reader Service — Here's How It Works:

Accepting your 2 free books and gift places you under no obligation to buy anything. You may keep the books and gift and return the shipping statement marked "cancel." If you do not cancel, about a month later we'll send you 3 additional books and bill you just $3.99 each in the U.S., or $4.74 each in Canada, plus 25¢ shipping & handling per book and applicable taxes if any.* That's the complete price and — compared to cover prices of $5.50 each in the U.S. and $6.50 each in Canada — it's quite a bargain! You may cancel at any time, but if you choose to continue, every month we'll send you 3 more books, which you may either purchase at the discount price or return to us and cancel your subscription.

*Terms and prices subject to change without notice. Sales tax applicable in N.Y. Canadian residents will be charged applicable provincial taxes and GST.

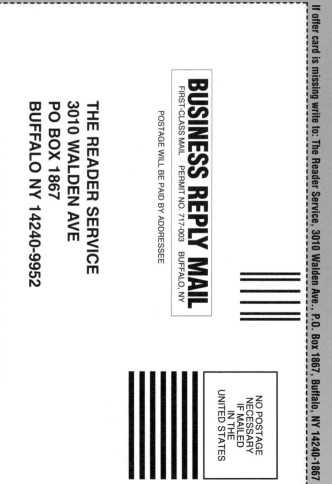

If offer card is missing write to: The Reader Service, 3010 Walden Ave., P.O. Box 1867, Buffalo, NY 14240-1867

BUSINESS REPLY MAIL
FIRST-CLASS MAIL   PERMIT NO. 717-003   BUFFALO, NY

POSTAGE WILL BE PAID BY ADDRESSEE

THE READER SERVICE
3010 WALDEN AVE
PO BOX 1867
BUFFALO NY 14240-9952

NO POSTAGE
NECESSARY
IF MAILED
IN THE
UNITED STATES

Jake felt as if he were on the edge of a rabbit hole, with the Mad Hatter and the Queen waiting at the bottom.

"The D word?" he said cautiously.

"Divorce."

She leaned close, close enough so her hair tickled his nose. Her curls were soft and smelled of vanilla. He could smell roses, too, maybe from her skin. It would be easy enough to find out. All he had to do was put his mouth against her throat and taste her.

"Don't look so shocked, Jake. Surely the concept is known here?"

"Concept? What...? Oh." He cleared his throat and moved back. "Yeah, sure. Divorce is the national pastime."

"Ah," she said, as happily as if he'd told her she'd won the lottery, and gave an excited bounce that made her breasts jiggle. *Didn't she have a bra on under that poor excuse for a sweatshirt?* "That's even better."

"It is?"

"Yes. Absolutely. See, divorce is frowned on in Brazil. Oh, it's legal, but it's mostly husbands who initiate the action, not wives. Even then, if you're in a certain social class, it's just not done."

Jake folded his arms. "Okay," he said, "let's have it. What kind of plot are you hatching?"

"It's simple, really."

Nothing about Catarina was simple. She'd made that abundantly clear.

"You find me a husband. A proper, eminently suitable Brazilian husband. You said you could do that, right?"

"Right," he said, as if it would be a snap. Well, finding a man to marry her would be, considering everything. Her money. Her looks. Her innocence.

Hell, her innocence. That was the thing that was going to make it tough. He couldn't just marry her off to anyone.

She'd need a special man, one who'd take time initiating her into—into—

"...hear me?"

Jake frowned. "Sorry. What did you say?"

"I said I'll marry the man of your choice. But before I do he'll have to agree to two conditions." She held up her hands. "One," she said, tapping her left thumb with her right index finger, "he'll have to sign a legal document giving up all rights to my inheritance."

"You're coming into a lot of money, Catarina. I don't think—"

"If you find me an eminently suitable husband, he won't need my money."

"'Eminently suitable' meaning rich."

"Disgustingly rich," she said brightly. "Weren't you going to do that anyway?"

"Well, I hadn't thought—"

"A man who's wealthy won't only want me for my money. Surely you'd figured that—or were you going to hand me over to just anybody?"

She was right. Jake sighed and nodded his head. "Okay. We need a man with lots of money. What else?"

"He has to agree that we remain here, in the United States."

"Cat. I don't know if a Brazilian would—"

"Third—"

"You said you had a couple of conditions. That means two."

"Third," she said blithely, "he has to sign documents agreeing ahead of time to a divorce. I'll marry him, I'll inherit my fortune, and then I'll file for divorce." Cat smiled. "Simple, isn't it?"

"Simple. Or simplistic. Why would a man agree to such a scheme? What's he going to get out of it? If you're thinking of dangling a cash reward in front of him, well, if this man has enough money not to want any of yours, why would he see cash as an inducement?''

This was it. The way to make her plan work. She didn't particularly like it, but what other out did she have?

''I thought about that.''

''And?''

Catarina took a deep, deep breath. Tough times called for tough measures.

''You have to realize,'' she said quietly, ''that I've been dreaming about my freedom for a long time.''

''I understand, but—''

''No!'' Cat put her hand on his forearm. ''No, Jake. You can't possibly understand. Not really. My parents died when I was very young. My uncle—my guardian—put me into the convent the day after the funeral and never took me out again. Not for holidays or summers or weekends. He left me there. It wasn't just my home, my school, it was my entire world.''

''Cat, it must have been awful, but—''

''It wasn't awful. Not all the time. Some of the sisters were good to me. I even made some friends. But when they turned eighteen they left. They went through those gates, Jake, the way I'd always thought I would. But I didn't. I had to watch them go while I stayed behind for another three endless years.'' Her fingers caught his shirt and twisted into it. ''The only thing that kept me from going crazy was dreaming about what it would be like when I finally walked through those gates, too.''

Jake could feel a tightness in his throat. His own childhood had been hit and miss. He'd courted danger and often found it, had his nose bloodied before he'd learned to throw the first punch to protect himself. But he'd had a mother who loved him and the city of New York as his playground, and when he'd turned eighteen he'd left the bad stuff behind forever.

The life Cat had just described sounded like the next best thing to doing hard time in prison.

He took her hand, clasped it between both of his.

"Cat," he said softly, "honey—"

"Don't you see?" Tears glittered in her eyes. "I can't spend the rest of my life in yet another cage, no matter how glossy it might be."

"I told you, I'll find a good guy. One who'll make you happy."

"Freedom will make me happy, Jake. Only freedom!" She took a shuddering breath. "I thought about giving up my inheritance—"

"No. You're not to do that. Your parents wanted you to have the money."

"I know. It's their legacy to me. And I know, too, that they thought they were doing the right thing, but—but—"

She began to weep. Jake cursed and pulled her into his lap.

"Don't cry," he said, holding her close against him. "Honey, don't. Please don't. I'll find a way."

Cat tilted her head back. "You will?"

"Yes. That guy at the Brazilian Embassy? I'll phone him tomorrow, ask him to introduce you around. To introduce *us* around. That way I can keep tabs on the men you meet. You'll have as much say in choosing the right one as I will."

"Thank you."

She smiled through her tears, swiped her hand under her nose. Jake freed one arm, reached past her for a napkin.

"Here," he said gruffly, holding it to her nose. "Blow."

She did. Then she gave a deep sigh and leaned against him, her head resting against his heart.

God, she was so warm. So delicate. She smelled so good, felt so good. One kiss. One little kiss, just to reassure her.

"Cat?" Jake whispered. He put his hand under her chin

and lifted her face until it was level with his. Her eyes grew big and dark; her lips parted. "Cat," he said hoarsely, and put his mouth against hers.

It was as if he'd kissed her a million times before. There was no hesitation, no cautious placement of lips and noses. The second their lips met, she sighed and opened her mouth to his.

"Jake," she whispered. "Jake…" And everything he'd promised himself about not kissing her fled his mind.

He was lost in her taste, her scent; he slipped his tongue between her lips and she gave another of those little moans, looping her arms around his neck, digging her fingers into his hair and holding on to him the same way he was holding on to her—as if the world were liable to stop spinning at any moment and all they had to keep from flying into space was each other.

Somehow, he shifted his weight.

Somehow, she shifted hers, until she was sitting astride him, until his hands were beneath that silly sweatshirt and, God oh, God, he'd been right. She wasn't wearing a bra.

Her breasts were wonderful to touch. Truly perfect. Warm and silken against his palms. Her nipples… God, her nipples begged for the heat of his mouth.

"Cat," he said thickly, and pushed up the damned shirt, bent his head, kissed the creamy slopes of her breasts, kissed the tips, drew one then the other between his lips, gently suckling, biting, tormenting her until she cried out in ecstasy, sobbed his name and moved, moved her hips, so that she was grinding her pelvis against his.

His erection was so hard it was almost painful. His body pulsed with life. With desire. With need for Catarina.

"Wait," Jake whispered, and he shifted her, clasped her hips, watched her face as he positioned her against him.

There were layers of clothing between them but it didn't matter. He could feel her muscles trying to close around him, see the blindness of passion in her eyes, hear the rasp of breath. Was it hers or his?

Nothing mattered but this.

This woman.

This moment.

This, this, this...

Jake groaned, cursed, pulled back.

"Jake?" Cat whispered.

He shuddered, shook his head, sat her on the other stool. His face was white, except for a vivid streak of color across each high cheekbone.

"Tomorrow," he said in strangled tones. "The Brazilian Embassy. I'll make that phone call, get some names..."

"Jake—"

She was staring at him, her eyes luminous, her skin glowing, her nipples tautly defined under the sweatshirt.

"I'm sorry," he said. "For everything."

"Not for this," she whispered. "Please don't be sorry for this."

Jake tried for an answer but couldn't find one. Instead, he rose from the stool and went to the door.

"I'll see you in the morning," he started to say, but Cat's voice cut across his.

"Jake?"

He stopped. Inhaled. Let out a long, slow breath. Where was the power of meditation when you really needed it?

"Yes?"

Cat's pulse was hammering; her bones felt liquid. How could she tell him the rest now, with her body aching for something she didn't really understand?

"About—about the husband you'll find me. The one who'll agree to a divorce."

Jake swung around and faced her. "Cat, I just told you. A man with enough money to agree not to touch yours—"

"—won't see any reason to go into a temporary marriage."

"Exactly."

"Am I pretty, Jake?"

His mouth twisted. "Catarina—"

"Just tell me the truth, okay?" She slid from the stool and walked toward him. "Am I pretty?"

"You know you are," he said, in a voice rough as gravel.

"And—and I'm untouched. I'm a virgin."

Did she think he didn't know that? It was all that had kept him from taking her a minute ago, from stripping her naked, cupping her hips, wrapping her legs around his waist.

"What's your point?"

"My point," she said slowly, "is that the man I marry will be my legal husband. For a day, a week, a month I'll be his wife. And..."

"And?"

"And," she said, forgetting her plan to be subtle. How could she be subtle with Jake looking at her like that? "And I'll give him the only gift he can't buy." She swallowed, forced moisture into her suddenly dry mouth. "I'll give him my virginity—and you're going to teach me how to do it."

CHAPTER EIGHT

WHAT response could a man make to a woman who had said something so outrageous?

Almost two weeks later, Jake sat at his desk in his office, still clueless. He had a million things to do—phone calls to make, appointments to keep, a stack of letters waiting for his signature—but how could he concentrate on any of them?

All he could think about was what Cat had asked him that night.

He picked up a pencil, tapped it mindlessly against the edge of the desk as he recalled how he'd stared at her, tongue-tied for the first time in his life.

"Jake?" she'd said, as calmly as if she were talking about the weather. "Did you hear me? Will you teach me about sex? Or is that going to be a problem?"

A problem?

Snap!

The pencil broke in half. Jake reached for another, began tapping again.

The question had been bad enough. The brilliance of how he'd dealt with it had been even worse. He'd firmed his jaw, narrowed his eyes, pointed his finger straight at her...

And told her to go to her room.

He groaned at the memory.

Go to her room. As if she were a child instead of a woman. When the fact was, Cat was every bit a woman. All he had to do was close his eyes and he could feel her straddling him again, her body molding itself to his, her nipples sweet against his tongue while she made those little sounds that could surely drive a man insane.

Tap, tap, tap.

He hadn't touched her again.

And she hadn't mentioned her crazy plan again. Maybe because he wouldn't give her the chance.

He came home each evening, said a polite ''hello'' and that was that. While they ate dinner he read through whatever he'd stuffed into his briefcase before leaving his office. Cat kept silent: he figured that had been the way meals were at the convent, and that was fine.

Dinner over, he excused himself, went up to his room and spent the rest of the evening there, working on his papers, catching up on his correspondence...

Jake swung his chair around and stared out the window.

Who was he kidding?

He didn't do anything even resembling work. He stared at the walls, at the TV screen, at the day's newspapers, at whatever might take his mind off the woman down the hall.

About how it was his responsibility to find her a husband.

About what she'd asked him to do.

How could she even suggest such a thing? He'd signed on to find her a husband, not to introduce her to sex— although the ugly truth was he'd come awfully close to doing exactly that.

But he'd been good the past two weeks. He hadn't touched Cat. And he'd kept his promise to phone the guy he knew at the Brazilian Embassy. He'd met Lucas for drinks, explained the situation...

Well, no. Not all of it.

Why go into the complicated details? That he'd inherited responsibility for the ward of the man who'd sired him, and that he was charged with finding her the right husband.

That her fortune and his future hung in the balance.

That Cat wanted to "buy" a fast divorce by offering the man who married her her innocence.

Snap.

Jake grabbed another pencil.

No, he hadn't told Lucas any of that. He'd just said the ward of a Brazilian acquaintance was staying with him and he wanted to introduce her to New York's closely knit Brazilian community.

"How old is the girl?" Lucas had asked.

Jake had told him. Lucas had nodded.

"There's a party at the Embassy next week."

Jake had felt as if a load were easing from his shoulders. "Great."

"Is she very unattractive?"

Jake had looked at Lucas. They were about the same age. Lucas was tall, dark-haired and he had a reputation as a ladykiller.

"If she were a ten," Lucas said, grinning over the frosted rim of his *caipirinha,* "I might just be interested—but she can't be, otherwise you'd keep her for yourself."

Jake tossed aside the pencil, rose from his chair and paced the length of his office. Keep Catarina for himself? What a ridiculous idea. She needed a husband. He needed to find one for her. And if she thought he'd school her in the things men and women did in bed before that could happen, she was out of her mind.

He turned sharply and paced in the other direction.

The only thing he'd teach her was how to be civil. The night he'd told her to go to her room she'd turned white with anger, called him something in Portuguese he figured was better left untranslated, and marched away.

A woman and a wildcat. That was what his supposedly demure ward had turned out to be. Mother Elisabete would probably vanish in a puff of smoke if she saw her charge now.

Especially in her new clothes.

That thought, at least, made him smile.

A few days ago he'd told Cat he was taking her to work with him so he could send her on a shopping trip with his personal assistant. Cat had responded with a glare. She was still angry because he hadn't agreed to enroll her in his personal version of Sex 101, but he'd ignored her sullen attitude.

It had been time to replace the South American version of Little Orphan Annie with a woman ready to face the challenges of New York.

Jake sat down again, tilted back his chair and folded his hands over his flat belly.

His P.A. had hardly blinked when he'd introduced Catarina as the daughter of a Brazilian acquaintance—the definition had worked with Lucas, so why not with Belle? He'd said he wanted Belle to take her to Saks or Henri Bendel and clothe her from head to toe.

Cat had stood in the center of the room, arms folded, eyes shooting sparks, but she hadn't argued. Maybe she'd finally realized that the things she kept pulling from her bottomless satchel weren't going to make it in Manhattan.

"Not Saks," Belle had said after she'd looked Cat over. "Not Bendel. Lauren, maybe. Calvin Klein."

"Whatever," Jake had replied impatiently. "I want the works. Clothes, shoes, makeup, jewelry—"

"A haircut?"

"No haircut."

There must have been something in the way he'd said it, because Belle had looked at him, brows raised as high as they'd go. He'd cleared his throat and mumbled a few words about Brazilian culture and long hair. A pathetic lie, but all he'd been able to come up with to get himself off the hook.

The truth was, he couldn't handle the idea of all that long, glorious hair ending up on the floor in some trendy salon when what he dreamed of each night was Cat lying beneath him in his bed, her mouth pliant under his, her hair streaming over his pillow as he made love to her...

"Hell," Jake said, and rose from his chair again.

Belle had done her job well. Cat had gone from beautiful to spectacular. When he'd entered the penthouse that night she'd greeted him at the door wearing jeans that fit her like a second skin, a sweater the same shade of coffee-brown as her eyes, spiky heels that had brought the top of her head almost level with his chin, and if her hair hadn't been cut then somebody had done something to it that had made the curls less wild and twice as sexy.

The sulky, imposed-upon expression had gone. For a change, Cat had been smiling.

"How do I look?" she'd asked, twirling before him.

Good enough to eat, he'd thought. Good enough to take in his arms and carry to bed.

"You look okay," he'd said briskly, and wondered if the lie was enough to make his nose grow. "You know, Catarina, I think I'll pass on supper. These reports..."

"I made our supper," she'd called as he started toward the stairs.

He'd turned and looked at her. "What about Anna?"

"I told her I wanted to cook tonight." She'd taken a deep breath. He'd seen that she'd worked up her courage for this. "It's Brazilian. Come and see."

That was when he'd noticed an unfamiliar scent in the air. She'd rattled off the name of something unpronounceable and looked at him with such hope in her eyes that he hadn't had the heart to refuse.

So he'd followed her to the kitchen, where she'd dipped a wooden spoon into a pot, held it out, said, "No, wait," and then brought the spoon to her own mouth, so she could purse her lips and gently blow on the steaming contents.

Watching her blow on that spoon had almost driven him to his knees.

"Now taste it," she'd said, and he'd wanted to—God, he'd wanted to...

Somehow, he'd gotten himself under control. Dragged his gaze from Cat's mouth to the spoon, let her slide it between his lips, fought the swift tightening of his body when she parted her own lips and poked out the tip of her tongue in unknowing parody of him. But not even his hottest fantasy had been enough to keep him from reacting to the taste of whatever it was she'd cooked.

"What is that?" he'd gasped.

"You didn't like it?"

"No! I, ah, I loved it. It's just—it's different," he'd said, and then he'd mumbled his lie about having work to do and fled.

Hours later, when even the street far below his apartment had gone quiet, he'd heard a faint sound. He'd told himself it was the wind, sweeping through the leafless shrubs on the terrace, but he had known damned well it was Cat, weeping. About his reaction to her cooking? He'd doubted it.

About his reaction to her request for help was more likely.

And he'd thought, *What if I went to her right now and said, Okay, you want me to teach you about sex? Here's lesson number one.*

He hadn't done it, of course. Lessons in seduction? In sex? If she thought he'd teach her what men and women did in bed, she was nuts.

Or was she?

In some way that danced on the edge of sanity he could almost see the logic of it. He relied on people he trusted to help him all the time: CPAs to do his taxes, lawyers to write contracts. Wouldn't it be better for Catarina to learn about sex from a man she knew and trusted than from a man she intended to marry and then divorce?

Jake sank down in the chair behind his desk again, picked up a pencil, rolled it mindlessly between his fingers.

There'd be a lot to teach her.

He'd start with the basics. How to let a man know she was interested. A little smile. A touch of her hand. No. She was innocent. He had to keep that in mind.

It would be best to start with what a man would do to her. That way none of it would come as a shock. She'd be prepared for what would happen.

He could do it tonight. Go home, confront Cat, tell her he'd decided to comply with her request. Say it just that way, so it sounded businesslike—because that was what it would be.

Businesslike.

Purposeful.

Instructions on how to make love.

He'd lead her to his room. Shut the door. Turn down the lights, leave just enough illumination so he could watch her face, see what pleased her when he touched her.

Undress her. Slowly. God, yes. Very slowly. Strip her naked, one garment at a time. And when she was naked, when she tried to shield herself from him, as she almost surely would, he'd take her hands in his.

Cat, he'd say softly, *sweetheart, don't. Let me look at you. You're so beautiful, Cat. Any man would give his soul to see you like this.*

Her eyes, those huge pools of darkest brown, would fix on his.

Tell me what pleases you, he'd say.

Then he'd reach out, touch her breasts. Her nipples. Watch them tighten in anticipation. A whisper of excitement would sigh from her lips, and when it did he'd cup her breasts, bend to them, suck the nipples into his mouth, tasting them on his tongue as he had that night in the kitchen.

She'd tremble with desire, but there'd still be fear in her eyes.

Do you like that? he'd ask.

And she'd say, *Yes, oh, yes, Jake. Oh, yes.*

Then he'd kneel down before her, stroke his hand down her belly, hear the swift intake of her breath as he cupped her hips, brought her closer and blew gently against the soft curls that guarded her virginity.

Jake, she'd sob. *Oh, Jake...*

Let me, he'd whisper, and he'd press his mouth to those curls, inhale her scent until the splendor of it made him dizzy. Her hands would be in his hair, clutching at him as she swayed, as he made her mindless with need.

That was when he'd scoop her into his arms, carry her to his bed, take her down and down onto the soft sheets, take off his own clothing, watch her eyes widen as she saw him naked for the first time.

Jake? she'd whisper unsteadily.

Shh, he'd say softly, *I won't hurt you. I'll never hurt you.*

He'd draw her against him, stroke her, soothe her, and when she finally relaxed he'd take her hand, kiss the palm, then bring it to his chest, let her feel his skin, let her measure the pounding beat of his heart as she'd tried to do that very first night in Rio.

See? he'd say. *There's nothing to be afraid of, Catarina.*

That pink tongue would peep out, touch her bottom lip in the way that drove him crazy. He'd force himself to hold still as she moved her hand over him, felt the heat of his skin, the softness of the hair on his chest, the flatness of his belly.

She'd hesitate then, her eyes filled with questions, and he'd clasp her hand in his again, gently move it down, grit his teeth against the need to plunge deep inside her as he felt her cool fingers close delicately around his hard, eager length.

She'd say his name, this time with a woman's need, and he'd cup her face, kiss her mouth, let his tongue enter its honeyed depths, and when she whimpered and began moving against him he'd say, *Yes, Cat, yes, sweetheart. This is what it's like to be with a man. A man who wants you more than he wants his next breath.*

And then he'd touch her.

Seek out that sweetness hidden between her thighs. Hear her cry out with passion as he opened her to him, as he sought out the delicate bud that had flowered just for him. He'd kiss her there, lick her until she writhed in his arms, and when she was lost, when she was sobbing his name and begging him to take her, then, only then, would he enter her, groan as he felt her exquisite heat, her tightness, close around him...

Snap.

The two halves of the pencil flew across the room.

None of that could happen. Taking Catarina's virginity would ruin her for another man. It would destroy her plan. He'd have to stop before he slid deep inside her, before he took her maidenhead, before he made her his, only his...

God!

Jake shot to his feet, turned to the window, leaned forward and touched his forehead to the cool glass.

What was he doing? He'd come within seconds of humiliating himself. How could that be? He was a grown man, years and years removed from a boy's game of sexual fantasy.

And why should he resort to his imagination when the real thing was readily available?

Jake grabbed the telephone and hit the button that connected him with Belle.

"Belle," he snapped, "call Miss Vickers. Tell her I'll pick her up for dinner. At seven-thirty."

"Miss Vickers?"

He heard the surprise in his P.A.'s voice. He couldn't blame her. He'd hardly spoken with Samantha since he'd returned from Rio, and then she'd been the one who'd made the calls.

"Yes, Miss Vickers."

"And if she's otherwise engaged?"

Was that a polite admonition or a reasonable question? Frankly, he didn't care.

"She won't be," he said, with the unknowing arrogance of a man who'd never had the least bit of trouble attracting women. "Then phone that place I was supposed to take her to last time."

"Sebastian's?"

"Right. Make a reservation for eight."

"Yes, sir." Belle hesitated. "What about Miss Mendes?"

"What about her?" Jake snarled, and slammed down the receiver.

Sebastian's was trendy and handsome, if you liked deliberately exposed copper pipes and cast-iron plumbing, steel beams and snaking electrical cables. The music was loud and fast; the too-small tables were jammed with Importantly Beautiful People and those who considered themselves Beautifully Important.

Samantha was stunning. Every man in the room watched her enter on Jake's arm; every man watched each time she laughed at his jokes, tossed back her mane of auburn hair and leaned forward to show off a cleavage that guaranteed she'd never drown should a flash flood mysteriously sweep through the city streets.

Except his jokes were lame. So was his conversation. All Jake could think about was Catarina, and how crestfallen she'd looked when he told her he was going out.

"With a woman?"

"Yes," he'd said, with almost deliberate cruelty. "With

a woman. But you won't be here alone. I called and asked Anna to stay for the evening.''

''I don't need a babysitter.''

He'd started to say that he knew that, that he'd asked Anna to stay just to keep her company, when he realized that she never had company in the evening—not with him safely ensconced behind the closed door to the master suite.

And then he'd thought, *Why did I use that word? Safely? Why would I need to feel safe in my own home?*

But by then Cat had stormed away, and the clock said he had less than forty minutes to shower and change and get downtown to Sam's. And now he was with Sam, and yet not with her, going through the motions of a date and stealing glances at his watch.

''…want to tell me, Jake?''

He blinked. Sam's artfully made-up face swam into focus. She was leaning over again, all that cleavage on display, but there was a sharp glitter in her eyes.

''Sorry. I, ah, I didn't quite hear what you said.''

''How could you? You aren't paying the least bit of attention to me.''

''Sorry,'' he said again. ''Business problems. You know how it is.''

''I *don't* know how it is. How could I? You don't call for weeks and then you ask me to dinner—and where are you?''

''Sam—''

''Is this a…'' She licked her lips. ''Is it, you know, a farewell meal? Because if it is, if you're breaking up with me—''

''No,'' Jake said quickly, ''it's not that. I've been… busy.''

''Busy doing what?''

He looked at her. Sam was sophisticated. Urbane. Maybe she could help him figure out the best way to deal with a woman who, until just two weeks ago, had lived a sheltered life.

He cleared his throat. "Someone—someone died."

"Oh, Jake—"

"Nobody I knew," he said hastily. "Just someone I have a connection to." He pushed his untouched plate aside. "It's complicated, but the bottom line is that I've been charged with a difficult responsibility."

"What responsibility?"

"I'm supposed to introduce a girl to society. Well, that's not entirely accurate. I'm supposed to introduce her to Brazilian society."

"Here? In New York?"

"Yes."

Sam frowned. Or would have frowned except for the Botox. Botox, at her age? He shouldn't have been surprised. When Sam frowned, when most of the women he knew frowned, they only managed to turn their eyebrows into caterpillars scaling their foreheads at a forty-five-degree angle.

Cat would never do that to herself. He knew it as surely as he knew she'd never spend half the time Sam had spent putting on her makeup tonight...

"Jake?"

He blinked again. "Yeah. Sorry."

"I asked you how old this child is."

"She's—" Whoa. Shaky ground. Why had he thought this would be something to discuss with Samantha? "You know what?" he said briskly. "Let's not bother talking about her. How about dessert? I know you're always counting calories, but—"

"How old is this child, Jake?"

"She's not exactly a child."

Sam's luminous eyes narrowed. "A teenager?"

Jake shook his head. "Not exactly."

"Then how old is she, *exactly?*"

"She's, uh, she's just past her twenty-first birthday."

Could a woman's eyes narrow more than that? Could she see out of them, if they did?

"She's a woman?"

"Yeah. More or less."

"More or less," Samantha said coolly. "And what does she look like?"

He knew what she meant. But that didn't make it mandatory to answer as if he did.

"Oh, I don't know. She's five-eight, maybe five-nine—"

"What does she look like, Jake?" Sam's voice took on a sharp intensity. "Is she attractive?"

Why in hell had he thought this conversation would be helpful? "I guess."

"You guess." Sam reached for her wineglass. "And where have you stashed her?"

Where was the waiter? It had to be getting late. To hell with dessert. Jake wanted the check. He wanted fresh air. He wanted to slice out his tongue.

"If you mean," he said cautiously, "where is Cat staying—"

"Cat?" Sam said, her voice as frigid as her slitted eyes.

"Catarina. She's, uh, she's staying at my place."

Silence. A long silence. After which Jake could have sworn he saw Samantha unsheath her claws.

"How charming. You have a woman living with you, and here you are having dinner with me."

"She isn't 'living' with me."

"No wonder I've spent the past hour talking to myself!"

"Take it easy, Sam."

"I should take it easy while you sit there, fixated on this—this—?"

"Sam." Jake's tone turned as cool as hers. "Watch what you say."

Samantha pushed back her chair. "I want to leave."

"We haven't finished our—"

"But we have. We've finished everything." Her mouth twisted. "To think of the time I wasted with you."

"Hey—"

"Wasted," she said bitterly, "with a man whose idea of decency is to pretend he's committed to one woman while he moves his—his paramour into his house."

Which charge should he answer first? Jake leaned forward. "She's not my paramour. And I never made any commitments, Sam. You know that."

"If you're thinking of turning this into a *ménage à trois,* forget about it, hotshot!"

"A *ménage à…*" Jake glowered at Samantha. "What the hell are you talking about?"

Samantha got to her feet. "Do us both a favor. Go home to your little Brazilian. It's obviously where you really want to be."

She strode past him toward the door. Jake pulled several bills from his wallet and dropped them on the table, then hurried after her. On the sidewalk, he caught her arm and turned her toward him.

"Just for the record, Catarina isn't my lover," he said quietly. "You know I'd never have asked you out tonight if she were."

The anger faded from Sam's eyes. "I know. It's just… She's a lucky girl, your housemate."

"Damn it, she's not—"

A taxi swooped to the curb. Sam broke free, ran to it and got in. Jake had just enough time to go after her and hand the driver a bill before the cab swung into traffic. He watched until it turned the corner. Then he took his cell phone from his pocket, started to punch in his driver's number, but changed his mind.

A cold drizzle was coming down. He turned up his coat

collar, dug his hands into his pockets and started walking slowly uptown.

Enough was enough.

Sam had it wrong. He owed her an apology for not being tuned in tonight, but it wasn't as if he hadn't wanted to be with her.

He hadn't been fixated on Cat, or that flash of pain in her eyes when he'd told her he was going out. He hadn't spent the evening wondering what she was doing, if she was thinking about him...

Hell.

He'd done this all wrong. Catarina Mendes didn't belong in his home. Tomorrow he'd move her out. Arrange for her to live in a hotel. Contact an agency and hire a companion to keep her company.

Tonight—tonight, he thought, his pace quickening, he'd have a serious talk with her. The Embassy party was only a few days away. She and he had to make some plans. Plans that made sense.

His job was to find her a suitable Brazilian husband. He'd do his best to find one. He'd do better than that. He'd find at least two candidates. She could pick the one she preferred. Then he could put this nonsense behind him, contact Enrique's attorney and tell him he'd sure as hell better tell him who his brothers were.

That, only that, was what mattered.

By the time Jake reached his apartment building he was almost smiling.

What was it the poet had said about the best-laid plans?

Jake tossed his keys on the marble-topped table near the door and found himself in the center of a tornado. He could hear voices upstairs, the sound of things hitting the floor, and there was an open empty shoebox lying in the foyer that looked like a coffin for some small alien being.

"Anna?"

No reply. The hair on the back of his neck rose.

"Cat?"

Nothing. Adrenaline buzzed through his veins. He dropped his coat on a chair and took the steps two at a time.

"Cat!" he roared. "Cat—"

Anna popped out of the guest suite, wringing her hands. "Oh, Mr. Ramirez, thank goodness!"

"What's happened? Where's Catarina? Is she—?"

Slam! Anna spun toward the bedroom; Jake shoved her behind him and bolted through the door to face the unknown.

To face...

Cat.

She was in the dressing room. She spun toward him, her cheeks bright pink, her hair in her eyes and her arms filled with shoes and purses and God only knew what else. Even as he blinked and tried to figure out what was happening, a couple of shoes tumbled from the stack and bounced against the parquet floor.

Those must have been the sounds he'd heard downstairs.

"Cat?" Jake took a careful step forward. "What's going on?"

"Miss Mendes is going out," Anna said. "I told her not to, that you wouldn't want her to, but she said—"

"She said?" Cat said hotly. "*I* said that I didn't need your permission!"

"She doesn't know the city," Anna said urgently. "I tried to tell her that, Mr. Ramirez, but—"

"Go out?" Jake took another step into the bedroom. It looked as if it had been torn apart. Dresses and little silk things he didn't want to look at too closely littered the bed; jewelry spilled from open boxes on the dresser. "Go where?"

"Someone phoned, sir. I was making dinner and—"

"And," Cat said, blowing her hair out of her eyes, "I picked up the phone." She gave Jake a chilly smile. "I thought it might be you, but it wasn't. It was a man named Lucas."

Jake felt his stomach drop. He turned to Anna and gave her what he hoped was a smile.

"Thank you, Anna. You can go home now."

"I can stay a little longer, Mr. Ramirez, if—"

"Home," he said firmly. He took out his wallet and pressed some bills into her hand. "Tell the doorman to call you a taxi."

Anna nodded. Jake waited until he heard the sound of the front door shutting. Then he cleared his throat and turned back to Catarina.

"What did Lucas say?"

"He asked to speak with you. I said you weren't home and he said—evidently he thought I was Anna—he said there was a party tonight, something last-minute, and if you wanted to come and bring along your Brazilian charity case—"

Oh, hell.

"Cat. It isn't the way it sounds."

"—bring along the lady you were trying to fix up so you could get her off your shoulders—"

"Back," Jake said absently. "Cat. Damn it, I swear I never said—"

"I am going to this party, Jake."

"No. I mean, not tonight. There's an Embassy function next week, and—"

'I—am—going," Cat said coldly. "I'll find myself a husband without your help, and I'll be off your shoulders once and for all."

"It's back," Jake said again. "And you're not on it. I never said—"

"Get out of my room, please. I want to finish getting dressed."

Finish? She was wearing a robe. She hadn't started dressing. But he decided not to risk things by pointing that out.

"I don't want you to go to this party, Catarina. You're not ready for it."

"No?"

"No."

"And why is that, pray tell?"

Jake rubbed the back of his neck. Why, indeed? Hadn't he come home prepared to tell her it was time things got moving? She had the clothes; Lucas had the contacts. But— but—

"I am going, and that's final."

A muscle tightened in his jaw. "Fine. You want to go to this party? We'll go together."

"I'd rather go alone."

"You'll have to get past me to do it."

Catarina opened her mouth to protest, but when she looked into Jake's eyes she changed her mind.

He looked as if he meant it.

CHAPTER NINE

A TASTE of freedom was a wonderful thing.

Catarina had spent years wondering what it was like to dress up, go out, dance and laugh and flirt—oh, yes, flirt. Nothing she'd imagined was as thrilling as the reality.

Jake had muttered that the little club all the way downtown was noisy and overcrowded. He was wrong. It was filled with life and pulsed with excitement. She loved it on sight. The DJ, the music, the strobe lights, the drinks—especially something called a *caipirinha* that looked like lemonade—well, limeade—and tasted like paradise and made you feel good, good, good.

Wonderful, all of it.

She was happy to see that the dress she'd bought with Belle was just right. Jake didn't like it. It was too short, too low, too everything. But he was wrong. She fit right in.

All the men who saw her liked it. She could tell by the way they looked at her. It made her feel good. Who cared what Jake thought when so many admiring glances came her way? He hadn't even asked her to dance with him.

Would it kill him to do something so simple?

Never mind. She didn't need Jake. The men here were—what was that American word? Hot. That was it. They were hot. One especially. Lucas Estero. Tall, dark and yum-yum. Lucas was gorgeous. Maybe not as gorgeous as Jake, but gorgeous enough.

Lucas had seemed shocked to meet her.

"This is Catarina?" he'd said to Jake.

"It is," Cat had replied, before Jake could answer.

Lucas's lips had curved in a smile. "Ramirez," he'd said

softly, "you sly fox." Then he'd taken her hand, brought it to his mouth, told her she was the most beautiful woman he'd ever seen—in Portuguese, of course—and she hadn't spoken another word to Jake since.

Jake had pulled out a chair at a table, where he still sat, arms folded, mouth set, eyes fixed on her, watching.

Let him watch. Let him notice that Lucas didn't seem to think she was a silly child. Lucas hadn't left her side. He introduced her to people, but he kept his arm around her waist in a way she hadn't quite liked at first, because it seemed too personal. But as the night wore on, and she danced and laughed and drank those deliciously sweet concoctions in tall, chilled glasses while Jake just sat there and glowered, Lucas's encircling arm felt more and more as if it belonged right where it was.

She didn't need Jake to pay attention to her. She had Lucas. Tall, good-looking and single Lucas.

She'd asked him that right away.

Lucas had grinned and touched his index finger to the tip of her nose. "*Querida,*" he'd said, "of course I am single. What kind of man do you think I am?"

The marrying kind, she'd thought. But fortunately she hadn't said it out loud. It was too soon to tell Lucas what she needed, and too soon to know if he was the right man for the job. Even if he wasn't, there were lots of men here tonight, virtually all of them Brazilian, young and good-looking. Not as good-looking as Jake, of course, but—

But who cared?

She certainly didn't.

Jake had nothing to do with her or her life except to find her a proper husband. He'd made it clear that was the only role he wanted. She'd asked him to teach her about men and sex and had he done it?

No. He had not.

He'd come close, that one time when they were in the

kitchen. Oh, God, so close! And it had been—it had been wonderful. The things she'd felt when he'd cupped her breasts, kissed them...

How could she have known it would be like that when a man and woman made love?

But then Jake had suddenly shoved her away, as if what they'd done was distasteful. He'd apologized for touching her when what she'd wanted was for him to go on touching her, go on kissing her, go on and on and never stop.

He'd hardly spoken to her since that night.

All he'd done was make it clear she was a burden that he wanted to get rid of. That was why he'd sent her shopping with his assistant, why he'd phoned his friend Lucas, why he'd made it a point to let her know he was involved with a woman...

"*Querida?* Are you okay?"

Catarina blinked. Lucas was looking down at her the way Jake never did, as if she were the center of his world.

"I'm fine," she said brightly. "Just—just maybe a little thirsty."

He grinned. "You like those *caipirinhas,* hmm? Didn't I tell you that you would?"

An hour ago she'd asked him what a *caipirinha* was. Lucas had slapped his hand over his heart.

"I'm shocked! A *carioca* who doesn't know what a *caipirinha* is?" Then he'd smiled and said once she tasted the drink she'd figure it out for herself.

She had. She'd tasted two, and they were quite obviously made from lime juice, sugar and ice.

Lucas kissed her hand. "Wait right here while I go to the bar."

Cat waited. While she did, she glanced over at Jake again. What was wrong with him? Didn't he know how to have fun? Couldn't feel the beat of the music?

Couldn't he see what Lucas saw? What her mirror confirmed? That she looked beautiful and sophisticated in her new dress of crimson silk? Her new spiky heels?

Didn't he want to tell Lucas to step aside, that he was the one who had the right to laugh with her, whisper to her, dance with—?

"Here you are, *querida*. Drink up."

She smiled up at Lucas, took the chilled glass he held toward her and drained it dry. She could almost feel the sugar course through her blood.

"Mmm. Delicious. Can I have another?"

"In a minute," Lucas said.

He took her empty glass and plunked it on a table. Then he led her onto the dance floor for a samba. She knew as little about the samba as she knew about *caipirinhas* and tried to tell him that, but he pressed his hand lightly in the small of her back and began to move. So did she. Before she knew it Lucas was grinning and she was laughing and everything was wonderful.

Let Jake sit there and glare. Let him watch. *Watch this,* she thought, and threw her arms around Lucas's neck.

"I love this dance!"

Lucas pulled her closer. "You dance as if you were born with the music of our people in your blood," he said, and gave her a little smile that made her breath catch.

The samba gave way to something slower and more sensual.

"A tango," Lucas said, drawing her tight against him. "Not Brazilian, but close enough."

"I don't know how to—"

"Relax. Feel how I move, *querida,* and your body will tell you the rest."

She could feel him, all right. His chest. His thighs. And could that possibly be his—his—?

"It's all right," Lucas murmured, his mouth at her ear. "Just let go and feel the rhythm."

He turned them in a slow circle. She had to twist her head to see if Jake was… Yes. He was. Still watching. Still stone-faced.

Why? He should have been delighted Lucas had invited them here tonight, that he seemed to have taken an interest in her.

The sooner Jake got her out of his life, the better. He'd made that absolutely clear.

Maybe he was in a bad mood because he'd quarreled with the woman he'd taken to dinner. Otherwise why would he have come home so early?

She didn't like thinking about that. About Jake with a woman. Not that she'd been foolish enough to think there weren't women in his life, but, really, couldn't he put them aside until he was no longer involved with her?

Not that he was exactly involved with her.

Not that he wanted to be involved with her.

He probably had all the sex he could handle with the woman he'd taken out tonight.

"*Querida,*" Lucas whispered, "relax."

What a mistake she'd made, asking Jake to be her teacher. He'd reacted as if she'd asked him to teach her about dental hygiene. Had her response to him that night been so awful? He'd seemed to like what they were doing…

Oh, Lord.

Maybe she'd overreacted. Was that it? Had she been too…? What was the word? Responsive? Receptive? How was a woman supposed to behave, when a man—?

"*Querida?* Are you having fun?"

Lucas's breath stirred her hair. Cat drew back in his arms and smiled brightly.

"Oh, I'm having a wonderful time!"

"I have the feeling Jake's been keeping you locked up."

"You're right."

"Well, he can't do it anymore." Lucas smiled. "Not now that I have the key."

The music changed again, this time to something even slower and softer. Lucas locked his hands at the base of her spine as they turned in a little circle. The room was starting to circle, too.

Cat closed her eyes and rested her forehead against Lucas's shoulder.

"Oooh," she said breathlessly, "I'm dizzy."

"You're probably thirsty from all this dancing," he said, his voice a little husky. He drew back, kept one arm tightly around her as he led her toward the bar. "Another *caipirinha* is what you need."

"What she needs is a pot of coffee and some aspirin."

Cat looked up. Jake was standing in front of them, his face dark as a thundercloud. It was so typical. The only thing he wanted to do was keep her from being happy.

"I don't want coffee and aspirin," she said defiantly. "I want another *caipa—caipa—*"

"No, you don't. We're going home."

Home? So he could go to his room while she went to hers? So she could sit in the dark and wonder what he'd done with that woman tonight that he wouldn't do with her?

"I don't want to go home. I'm having fun."

"She's having fun," Lucas said. "And I can see that you aren't. Go home, Jake. I'll take care of Catarina."

"Yeah," Jake said coldly, "I'll bet you will." He wrapped a hand around Catarina's wrist. "She's leaving, Estero, and so am I."

"Don't talk about me as if I'm not here," Cat said angrily. "I am not leaving. Lucas doesn't think I should go home yet. Isn't that right, Lucas?"

"Lucas's opinion doesn't mean a damn," Jake growled. "If I say you're leaving, you're leaving."

"I am not!" Cat dug in her heels. "Lucas, tell this man he doesn't run my life."

"You heard the lady," Lucas said, but Jake could hear the uncertainty in his voice.

"Did I ever get around to telling you why Cat's in New York with me, Estero?" Jake's smile glittered. He leaned in, as if he were about to share a great secret. "She's husband-hunting."

Cat's breath hissed through her teeth. "Jake! This is not the time to—"

"The lady you've been teaching the tango can teach you a thing or two, pal. I mean, you'd never know she's here to snare a husband, would you?"

"Jake!"

"The guy's qualifications have to be only that he's Brazilian, breathing and rich. Well, and single, of course. Right, Cat?"

Lucas had a funny look on his face. "Is this true?"

He spoke to Catarina, but it was Jake who answered.

"Absolutely true. And you, my man, are eminently qualified in all categories."

Cat felt the sting of angry tears in her eyes. Why was Jake doing this to her? She'd been having fun for the first time in longer than she could remember. Lucas, the music, the delicious whatever-they-were-drinks sliding so easily down her throat...

She looked at Lucas. "It's not the way he makes it sound. I wasn't— I didn't—"

"She asked if I was single," Lucas said to Jake. He shuddered, like a spaniel coming in from the rain. "But she never said—"

"No," Jake said, "I'm sure she didn't."

Cat swept her gaze from one man to the other. She hated them both, but Jake most of all. Hated him, hated him, hated—

"Time to say goodnight, Catarina."

She jerked against his hand. He tightened his grip until she gasped.

"You son of a bitch!"

"Such language," Jake said with an icy smile. "What would Mother Elisabete think?"

"Let go!" Cat demanded, banging her fist against his back as he dragged her to the door. "Damn you, Jake Ramirez!"

People laughed, stepped aside, let him pass through, hauling her in his wake. He paused beside the table he'd occupied, picked up her coat and his, then resumed his march through the club to the street.

The rain had turned to snow. Another time Catarina might have turned her face up to its cool bite. She'd never seen snow before, except in an old movie, but for now her rage was all-consuming.

Jake stopped, swung her toward him. "Put your coat on."

"I don't take orders from you!"

"Put the coat on," he growled.

Rebelliousness glittered in her eyes. He cursed, drew the coat around her, snatched it before it could hit the pavement when she flung it off, and cursed again.

"If you get pneumonia and end up in my life for an extra few weeks, so help me I'll—"

"You'll what? You're stuck with me, Ramirez, the same as I'm stuck with you."

She was right, damn it, even if he didn't want to hear it. And where the hell was Dario? He'd phoned his driver before he'd started across that snakepit of a dance floor— phoned him as soon as he saw what Lucas was up to.

Hell, he'd known what Lucas was up to sooner than that, but he'd figured, okay, this was Catarina's show, she was the one on a husband-hunt. Let her do things her own way.

But there was only so much a man could take of watching such a piss-poor seduction.

Lucas, with that slippery smile. Lucas, pouring drinks that tasted harmless but had the kick of a mule down Cat's throat. Lucas, supposedly teaching her to dance just so he could get her into his arms, his hands all over her, touching her, caressing her.

Lucas, just waiting for the chance to get Cat alone so he could undress her, feel the heat of her flesh against his, feather his thumbs across her nipples until she cried out.

Lucas had no right to do any of that because Cat belonged to—she belonged to—

"Mr. Ramirez?"

Jake jerked his head around. His car was at the curb; Dario stood on the pavement next to the open passenger door, his face a polite blank, as if seeing his boss wrestling a woman into submission was an everyday occurrence.

Jake started toward the car. Cat didn't.

"Walk," he said grimly.

"I told you, I don't take orders from—"

Her protest ended in a shriek as Jake picked her up, carried her to the car and unceremoniously dumped her inside. Then he got in beside her, folded his arms over his chest and shut his ears to the names she called him all the way home.

One good thing about having a penthouse high up in a fancy building on Fifth Avenue.

You were guaranteed a terrific view, no matter what the season.

Even winter.

At twenty minutes past two in the morning, wearing a pair of old sweats, Jake stood on the terrace that wrapped around his apartment. A mug of coffee steamed between his hands; his breath was a plume of smoke in the cold air. The snow, mantling the park in pristine white, had stopped.

It was a beautiful sight. At least, he supposed it was.

He was still too angry, too upset, too everything to keep his mind on anything as mundane as the weather.

He'd made a load of mistakes tonight—starting with losing his temper when he'd come home and found Catarina getting ready to go out, and ending with a repeat performance when he'd realized Lucas was coming on to her.

Coming on to her? Jake snorted. Lucas had been all over her, the miserable son of a bitch. And instead of taking him by his collar, hauling him outside and teaching him a lesson about how to treat a woman, a young and innocent woman, he'd let it all out on Cat.

He'd been wrong. Dead wrong. Taking her to that club, handing her over to Lucas, had been pretty much like putting a lamb in a cage with a hungry lion.

What in hell had he been thinking?

Jake took a sip of coffee.

He hadn't been thinking. That was the problem. Coming home, finding her all excited at the prospect of meeting a man, had ticked him off. What was her rush? He'd said he'd find her a husband, hadn't he? Instead she'd decided to start the search on her own. And he'd thought, okay, she wanted to play in the big league? Let her see how far she could get without him to take care of her.

Pretty far, as it had turned out. Lucas had taken one look and wanted what he saw.

What man wouldn't?

Trouble was, Cat didn't know the first thing about handling an operator like Lucas. How could she? That was why she'd asked Jake for help.

Teach me, she'd pleaded. And he'd responded by ignoring her.

Jake finished his coffee, put the mug down and leaned on

the railing again. He'd turned his back on her request and look what had happened. Okay, he didn't want to teach her how to make love, but still he could have sat her down, talked to her. Explained the facts of life.

How men could smile and seem sincere. How they could seem friendly and harmless. How they could make her laugh. When all the time what they really wanted was to get her into bed.

Even tonight he'd behaved stupidly.

She'd wanted to dance? He could have danced with her instead of letting Lucas teach her how it felt to be in a man's arms. He could have been the man who made her laugh.

He liked the way she laughed, the way she tossed her head so that her hair cascaded down her back.

And that night when she'd asked him to teach her about sex.

He could have said yes. Yes, I'll teach you.

He could have taken her to bed, lost himself in her, made love to her until she sighed with pleasure and understood that the touch of a man's hand...

Hell, no.

Until she understood that the touch of *his* hand, only his, could make her whisper *Jake, I want you. Jake, I need you. Jake...*

"Jake?"

He swung around. Cat stood in the open doorway, but her soft whisper had nothing to do with passion. She was wrapped in a robe that looked as if she'd swiped it from a barn; her face was pale and shiny with sweat despite the cold.

"Cat?"

"Jake," she moaned, "I'm going to be—"

He scooped her into his arms, carried her through the darkened rooms to the closest bathroom and got her there with no time to spare.

"It's okay," he said, holding her as she bent over the commode. "It's okay, honey."

She was violently ill, but he knew it was for the best. She'd feel better once her stomach had rid itself of the rum in the loathsome *caipirinhas*. When she was done, he gave her water to rinse her mouth, gently washed her face, then carried her up the stairs to her room and sat her on the edge of the bed.

She was shivering with cold. Gently, he slipped his hand under the collar of the heavy robe and touched her throat. She was soaked with sweat.

"Cat. You have to change your clothes."

"I feel awful." Her voice was so soft he could hardly hear her. "My stomach hurts. And my head. Oh, God, Jake, I want to die!"

"Let me help you change out of this wet stuff. Then I'll bring you something that will make you feel better."

"Promise?"

He had to smile. "Cross my heart."

He pressed a kiss to her forehead, went to her closet and rummaged through it. He found a long flannel nightgown in one of the built-in drawers and brought it to her.

"Come on, honey. Stand up so I can get this robe off you."

With his help, she wobbled to her feet. He undid the sash of the robe and wondered where in hell Belle had taken Cat shopping that she could have found something so ugly.

"...self," Cat mumbled.

"What, sweetheart?"

"I said," she told him as he eased the thing from her shoulders, "I know how horrible this robe looks, but I kept it 'cause—"

"Ah. I understand. You made it yourself."

"Yes. And it always made me feel better when I was

sick, or when I was unhappy.'' She made a little sound that
was more a sob than a laugh. ''Silly, huh?''

Jake's throat tightened. ''Not silly at all,'' he said, pic-
turing her in that convent school, alone and desperate and
wrapped in the next best thing to a horse blanket for com-
fort.

She swayed unsteadily as the robe fell away. He swept
one arm around her; she sighed, leaned forward and
slumped against him. She was wearing a flannel nightgown
under the robe. The gown was damp. He could feel each
soft curve of her body as she rested in his embrace.

''Honey.'' He cleared his throat. ''You need to get out
of this gown and into a dry one.''

'''kay.''

He looked down at her. Some color had come back to her
face but her eyes were closed.

''Shall I—shall I help you?''

''Umm.''

He took a deep breath. ''Lift your arms, sweetheart.
That's my girl. A little higher. Good. Great.''

Great? The hell it was. He did the best he could, kept his
eyes fixed on a point in space, but he had to glance at her
to get the fresh gown over her head, to get her arms through
the sleeves. And God, dear God, she was beautiful, so beautiful, so delicately boned and sweetly fleshed. But he didn't
feel passion or desire as he looked at his Cat.

He felt—he felt...

Jake swallowed hard. ''Okay,'' he said briskly. ''Time to
get into bed.''

Cat slumped down on the foot of the mattress. Jake lifted
her in his arms, carried her to the side of the bed and drew
back the covers. He started to lay her down, then thought
better of it. The sheets and pillowcases were probably damp.

''Honey?''

''Hmm?''

"Can you stay awake long enough for me to change the linens?"

"Mmm."

"All you have to do is sit here. I'll come right back with fresh ones, and with that drink that'll make you feel better."

"Mmm."

"Cat?"

"Mmm," she whispered, and buried her face against his throat as she linked her heads behind his head.

Jake froze. She felt so right in his arms. So fragile. So vulnerable. He turned his face, touched his lips to her hair and closed his eyes.

"This is all my fault," he murmured. "I'm sorry, sweetheart. I should never have abandoned you."

She sighed again. One last soft brush of his mouth and then he'd put her down... Except she wouldn't be able to sit here while he went to the linen closet for sheets, to his kitchen for ingredients for the concoction he recalled from his college days.

She could sleep in his bed.

He could sleep on the lounge in his dressing room.

She'd be warm and safe, and he wouldn't have to worry about her getting up during the night and being sick again without him to take care of her.

He carried her down the long hall from her bedroom to his, sat her on the edge of his oversized bed, knelt before her and clasped her hands.

"Stay awake," he said. "Okay? Just a couple of minutes more. Can you do that for me, Catarina?"

He hurried into the kitchen, put together the noxious drink that would cure her. By the time he got back she was slumped against the pillows.

"Not yet, Sleeping Beauty." He sat beside her, put his arm around her shoulders, brought the cup of horror to her lips. "Drink."

Cat swallowed. Her eyes flew open. "Ugh!"

"I know, honey, but it'll make you feel better. I promise."

She looked at him. Then she parted her lips and let him feed her the rest of the stuff. A muscle knotted in his jaw.

She trusted him. Only God knew why.

"Okay," he said, when she shuddered. "All done. Now, lie back. That's my girl. Get under the covers. Good. Just close your eyes—"

She whispered something. Jake bent closer.

"What?"

"I said, I'm sorry. I didn't mean to make you mad."

Again, that sudden tightness in his throat. "I'm the one who's sorry, Catarina. I should never have left you alone with Lucas. Can you forgive me?"

Two tears snaked down her cheeks. She closed her eyes and turned away.

"It's my fault. You told me not to go. I should have listened."

"Cat." Jake cupped her face. She was weeping quietly and it broke his heart. "I want you to get some sleep. Will you do that for me? We can talk about this in the morning."

After a moment, she nodded. "All right."

"Good girl." He bent closer and kissed her forehead. "If you need me—"

"Don't go."

"I won't go far. I'll be right next door."

She opened her eyes, looked at him and put her arms around his neck.

"Stay with me, Jake," she said softly. "Please."

"Cat. Honey—"

She was asleep. All he had to do was take her hands from his neck and fold them over the blanket.

Instead, Jake did what he'd wanted to do since they'd

reached New York. He got under the covers and took her in his arms.

She sighed and burrowed against him, and he marveled at how right it felt to hold her exactly like this.

Locked together, hearts beating as one, they slept until just before dawn, when a whisper of sound woke Jake from sleep.

It was Cat, looking into his eyes and saying his name, saying it as he'd longed to hear it since he'd first kissed her.

"Jake," she sighed, "Jake…"

"Cat," he said huskily, and took her mouth with his.

CHAPTER TEN

MAYBE Jake's kiss was part of her dream.

The images were already fading away, but Catarina remembered enough to know that she'd dreamed she was in Jake's arms.

In Jake's bed.

She touched his face. Smoothed his dark hair back from his forehead and whispered his name.

"Yes," he said. "Yes, sweetheart." And that was when she knew the dream was over.

This was real.

Jake, holding her close, his arms hard around her. Jake, his mouth on hers, tasting her, letting her taste him.

Yes, oh, yes, oh, yes!

Cat said his name again, her lips curving in a smile, and looped her arms around his neck. He groaned, kissed her another time, but then he clasped her hands and tried to draw them down.

She wouldn't let it happen.

The near-darkness, the intimacy of the bed, of his kisses, made her bold.

"Don't stop," she murmured. "Please, Jake. I've waited so long for you to do this...don't stop now."

She felt his body shudder against hers.

"Cat," he said hoarsely. "Honey, this isn't a good idea. I shouldn't have kissed you. Hell, I shouldn't have taken you to my bed, but you were sick and I wanted you close, where I could take care of you."

"You've done that all along. Taken care of me, I mean."

"I haven't," he said. She could hear the anger in his

voice. "I've been awful to you, Cat." He cupped her face, stroked the tangled curls back from her face. "Taking you out of that school without any real explanation," he said, his tone softening. "Making you to fly to the States, ignoring you once you were here, acting as if I hated having you around when the truth was—the truth was—"

"What?" Her voice was barely a whisper. "What was the truth, Jake?"

What, indeed? He was a man who'd been going along a road, traveling contentedly from point A to point B, and then Cat had come along and changed everything. She'd turned his existence upside-down and he'd complained about it. To her. To himself. She was trouble, he'd said. She was a burden.

The truth was that she was the best thing that had ever happened to him. She was more than he'd ever dreamed he'd find, and she could never be his.

"The truth," he said roughly, "is that you're wonderful—and I've wanted you from that first night in Rio."

"Then take me," she said softly. "Make love to me, Jake."

He took her hand, brought her palm to his lips and kissed it. "I—I can't."

"But you just said—"

He silenced her with a kiss so deep that she was trembling when he ended it.

"I want you more than I've ever wanted anything in my life. But I can't take your virginity, sweetheart. It would be wrong."

"It would be right," Cat said fiercely, and as she said the words she suddenly knew the truth.

She loved Jake with all her heart.

She knew better than to tell him that. Fate had brought them together; reality would drive them apart. But she could tell him some of what she felt.

She had to tell him that much.

"Jake," she said softly, "don't you see? Making love with you will be the one thing, the only thing, I'll have to remember when—when we're not together anymore."

Jake drew a shuddering breath and tried to close his ears to what she was saying. Instead, he gathered her against his heart, held her, rocked her... And then he groaned and kissed her with all the emotion he'd so carefully kept hidden.

From Cat.

From himself.

"Tell me what you like," he said. "When I touch you... Tell me."

"Anything you do. Any place you touch—"

Her head fell back as he put his open mouth against her throat. She tasted like wild honey; her scent made his head spin.

A surge of emotion he'd never felt before shot through him.

"Cat," he whispered. It was all he trusted himself to say. There was more, the words just out of reach, but for now her name was enough. He said it again as he ran a gentle finger over the taut outline of her nipple beneath the cotton fabric of her gown, then sucked it into his mouth.

A wild sob of pleasure burst from Cat's throat. She clasped Jake's head, her fingers tunneling into his hair as she arched against him.

Her body was on fire. Her breasts tingled. She could feel liquid heat between her thighs, in that place Sister Angelica had once said was the ultimate source of evil.

She wanted to feel Jake's hand there. Between her legs. Was she evil, too, for wanting such a thing? It didn't matter. She couldn't ask. She'd never—

She didn't have to.

His hand slid under her nightgown, his callused fingers deliciously rough against her ankle. Her calf. Her knee.

Cat grabbed his wrist.

"Jake?" she said shakily. "Oh, God, Jake…"

His hand stilled. She felt his entire body tighten.

"Cat," he said hoarsely. "Honey, if you want me to stop, tell me now."

She stared at him for a long moment. Then she touched a hand to his cheek.

"Don't stop," she said, her voice so low he could hardly hear it. "I want—I want you to touch me everywhere. I need—I need—" Her breath caught. "Don't hold back. Do everything. Show me everything. That's what I want, Jake."

The whispered plea raced through him like a flame touched to kindling. Jake cupped Cat's face and kissed her hard, slanting his mouth over hers again and again. He nipped her bottom lip, sucked it into his mouth, groaned when he felt the first, delicate slide of her tongue against his.

The last bonds of restraint slipped away.

There were tiny buttons down the front of her old-fashioned nightgown. Putting it on her hours ago, he hadn't trusted himself to deal with all those buttons. Instead, he'd slipped the gown over her head.

It turned out he couldn't deal with them now, either. His fingers felt too big, too clumsy. With a growl, Jake hooked his fingers into the demure neckline and tore it open down to her waist. He dipped his head, kissed her breasts, licked her honeyed pink nipples.

Cat went wild in his arms. Her head thrashed against the pillow; her hair slid over it like silk. How many times had he imagined this? Cat in his bed, his name spilling from her lips as he made love to her?

He kept his eyes on her face as he cupped her breasts and feathered his thumbs over the tips. She cried out; her dark lashes fell to her cheeks, flushed the pale rose of a shell tossed on the shore by a storm.

She was beautiful. So beautiful.

And she was his.

He kissed her mouth, swallowing her soft cries of pleasure. He swept his hand down her warm flesh to her narrow waist and slid his fingers under the torn nightgown. His blood was roaring in his ears. A huge wave was building inside him; the need for release pounded through his body with each beat of his heart.

He wanted to tear away the rest of the nightgown. Rip off his clothes. Bury himself deep in Cat's warmth.

He couldn't.

It was her first time. And, in some way he couldn't understand, it was his first time, too.

He wanted it to be perfect.

Jake took a deep breath. Forced himself to slow down. To undo the remaining buttons of the nightgown one by one, then fold back the edges. She was naked now, his Catarina, completely exposed to his eyes.

God, she was so lovely! Her skin was the color of richest cream; the curls that guarded her innocence were a soft whorl of chestnut and gold.

He kissed her belly. Her navel. Slid his hands beneath her and lifted her to him.

"Jake?" Her voice shook.

She said his name again as he moved lower, kissing his way down to those curls. Suddenly she reared up, hands outstretched to stop him. He caught her wrists, kissed her fingers, eased her back against the pillows.

"I want to taste you, Cat."

She shook her head. "No. It's wrong. You mustn't—"

"How can it be wrong for me to worship you with my body?" He bent down, kissed her eyes, her mouth, her breasts. "Every part of you is beautiful, sweetheart. This part, this hidden flower, is the most beautiful of all, because it belongs only to me. To me, Cat. To—''

She cried out as he opened her to him, stroked the delicate flesh within, then put his mouth to her. She half rose off the bed; she fell back, sobbing with pleasure. He knew she was afraid of what he was making her feel, but she didn't have to be.

She would fly into the sun and he'd be there to catch her, safely in his arms.

Jake lifted his head. Kissed her mouth. Let her taste their commingled passion on his lips.

"Let go," he whispered. "Do it for me, sweetheart. Just let go."

"I can't," she said brokenly. "I can't. Jake—"

He kissed her again, slid his hand between her thighs and stroked her, and all at once she cried out and shuddered in his arms.

"Jake," Cat said, and she broke free of the earth, of the emptiness that had been her life.

Jake said her name. Entered her. Sank deep, deep into her silken heat.

She felt one quick, sharp pain.

After that there was only ecstasy.

She must have fallen asleep.

It didn't seem possible, not after what had happened, but the next time she opened her eyes, Jake's arms were tight around her, her head was on his chest, and the room was filled with a strange white light.

"It's the snow," Jake said softly.

She tilted her head and looked up at him.

"The light. It's because of the snow. It must have started again during the night. It's still coming down." His lips curved in a smile. "Good morning."

She knew she was blushing. It was silly, but she couldn't

help it. "Good morning," she whispered, and buried her face against his throat.

"Are you okay?"

Her color deepened. Thank goodness he couldn't see it. "I'm fine."

"If I hurt you—"

"You didn't. Really. I wanted— I wanted—"

Jake put his hand under her chin and gently lifted her face until her eyes met his.

"So did I," he said huskily.

Her lips curved in a smile. He smiled, too, and gave her a tender kiss. After a long moment he cupped her shoulders and eased her down against the pillows.

"Don't go anywhere," he said softly. "I'll only be a minute."

Cat tugged the blankets to her chin as he got to his feet. It was the first time she'd really seen him naked, the first time she'd seen any man naked, and she drank in the sight as he strolled to the connecting bathroom.

How beautiful he was! Broad-shouldered, narrow-hipped, long-legged. He had a tight bottom, and she blushed again as she wondered how he'd look from the front. She'd felt him, deep, oh, so deep within her, but she hadn't actually seen...

"Here we go."

She blinked. He'd tied a towel around his middle. Too bad, she thought, and again the hateful color spread into her face. But before she could feel too stupid Jake was at the bed, scooping her into his arms.

"What are you doing?"

"Taking care of you," he said, and brushed his lips over hers.

"Taking...?" She glanced back at the bed. This time she was sure she turned pink, from the top of her head to her toes. There was a red stain on the white sheets. Mortified, she dug her face into the juncture of his neck and shoulder.

"Oh, God," she moaned. "Jake, I'm sorry. I'm such an idiot—"

"Sorry? For giving me such a gift?"

He kissed her hair as he carried her into the bathroom. A stream of water splashed from a gold faucet into an enormous black marble tub. Jake stepped into it, Cat still safe in his arms. He sat back, kept her nestled against him, and she sighed with contentment as the scented water lapped at her breasts.

"Sweetheart, if anyone should be apologizing it's me. I took something precious from you last night."

"You took something I wanted to give you," she said, turning so she could see his face. "Only you," she whispered, and she shocked herself, shocked him, by reaching for him, taking his already erect penis in her hands and stroking its silk-over-steel length.

"Cat," Jake said tightly, "honey, it's too soon..."

"It isn't," she said, and he slid into her and made love to her with his body and, heaven help him, with his heart.

How had it happened? How had he fallen in love with his ward?

A couple of hours later, bundled in sweats and heavy socks, mittens and woolen caps, they stood on the terrace and looked at a city turned into a fairyland by snow.

At least Cat was looking at the city.

Jake was looking at her, and trying to find a way out of the nightmare that trapped him.

He was in love with Catarina.

And he had to marry her off to another man.

Otherwise he'd violate the terms of both wills. Her parents', and his father's. She'd lose her inheritance. He'd never learn the names of his brothers.

"Oh, look," she said, with a little squeal of delight. "Jake? That man is skiing. Skiing—on Fifth Avenue!" She turned to him, eyes bright with excitement. "Isn't this wonderful?"

"Wonderful," he said.

What was wonderful was his Cat. How could he give her up? She was all a man could hope for, and more.

Everything was so new for her today. She'd never seen snow until the other night, and now New York had obliged with an honest-to-goodness blizzard that had brought the whole city to a standstill.

She'd never been with a man before, either, and he'd obliged by taking her innocence.

He'd had no right to it but, damn it, he had no regrets. Making love with her had filled him with happiness. She was amazing. She'd held nothing back; she'd given him everything. Her joy at being in his arms. Her passion. Her sweetness.

He'd imagined what it would be like to make love with Cat but nothing he'd fantasized compared with the reality of making her his.

Except she wasn't his. She couldn't be.

"Jake, do you see that? That woman with the big black dog? Oh, he's adorable! He's trying to bury his muzzle in the snow."

"I see it," he said gruffly, tightening his arm around her, but in truth what he saw was what had to happen next. The men he'd have to introduce to Catarina. The search he'd have to organize so that he found her the proper husband.

Pain, sharp as a surgical blade, sliced through his heart.

No. He couldn't do it. How could he let her give herself to another man to meet the terms of two wills that should never have been written? How could he see her with that man and know that she'd never be his again?

"Jake?" She swung toward him, eyes wide and shining. "Could we go to the park and make a snowman?"

No. Hell, no. The only place he wanted to go was back to bed, to stay there forever, make the real world go away until it was just Cat and him.

"I know it's still snowing, but please could we?"

He swallowed and managed a smile. "Sure we could, honey," he said, but first he took her back to bed and made love to her again.

She was enthusiastic, insatiable and inexhaustible—in bed and out.

All of it was catching.

They didn't build a snowman; they built a snow family. They'd raided the fridge before they went downstairs, so they made a guy with a carrot for his nose, a lady with half a cucumber for hers, a little round blob of a snow baby with a pair of radish eyes and another blob, smaller and squatter, that Cat solemnly christened Lassie.

Maybe you couldn't change the future, but on a magical day like this you could keep reality at bay.

"Lassie?" Jake grinned as she put the finishing touch to the mounded snow. "What could you possibly know about that collie? She hasn't made a movie in years."

"I know that 'she' was a 'he,'" Cat answered primly. "And I saw a whole bunch of Lassie movies. The school ran them on Friday nights."

"Along with lots of other smash hits, I'll bet."

"You're just jealous because I got to watch old movies."

Jake's smile tilted. "I'm just jealous because you got to watch them without me."

Cat stood up and moved closer. "You know what I always wanted to do?" she asked. A smile—a teasing, sexy smile—curved her mouth. She rose on her toes so her lips were almost at his ear. "I always wanted to watch movies in bed."

His body reacted with such speed he was glad there was nobody near enough to notice. He reached out, slid his arms around her and pulled her against him.

Her little gasp of surprise told him *she* noticed, but that was exactly what he'd intended.

"Then this is your lucky day," he whispered. "I just happen to have a DVD player, as well as a bed."

"You do?"

Cat batted her lashes. She'd gone from innocent virgin to tempting vixen in a heartbeat, and he was crazy about both of them.

"Yeah. I do." He bent his head and gave her a lingering kiss. "And, if you're a very good girl, I'll show them to you."

"How about if I'm very bad?" she said, and her cheeks turned such a shade of crimson that he began to laugh.

"Oh," she whispered, hiding her face against his shoulder, "what would Sister Angelica say?"

"I know what *I'd* say," Jake replied.

He bent down, put his mouth to her ear and whispered something. She looked properly shocked. She also looked properly delighted.

Jake grinned, plucked her off her feet, ignored her shrieks as he tossed her over his shoulder, and trotted out of the park, across a still-unplowed Fifth Avenue, past the bemused doorman and up to his apartment, where her supposed outrage ended.

"Cat," he whispered, "my sweet kitten."

Hours later, as he lay with her sleeping in his arms, Jake wondered how in God's name he was ever going to give her up.

And then he thought, with sudden clarity, *I don't have to give her up.*

What he had to give up was his right to the names of his brothers.

Suddenly that didn't seem half as important as what he'd already found, right here in his arms.

He felt a surge of joy so powerful it made him grin…and then his grin faded.

He knew what he wanted, but the choice had to be Cat's.

For all he knew, her inheritance—the freedom and the independence it represented—meant more to her than he did.

Cat woke alone.

Jake was gone. So was the storm. The snow had stopped falling and the city must have been plowed, because she could hear the sounds of night-time traffic.

Life was returning to normal. Why was the thought so depressing?

She pushed aside the blankets and sat up. Her clothing was everywhere. Bits and pieces lay on the floor—they hadn't made it all the way to the bed before Jake began undressing her.

Before they began undressing each other.

She'd been as eager to strip him naked as he'd been to strip her. She loved feeling his skin against hers, loved seeing his strong male body, loved…loved—

Cat swallowed hard and got to her feet. The robe Jake had bundled her into early this morning, after he'd bathed her, was draped across the back of a chair. She put it on, rolled up the sleeves, tied the sash securely at her waist and started down the hall to her rooms.

"Supper's almost ready."

She spun around. Jake stood at the foot of the stairs, looking up at her. He was wearing jeans and a dark blue sweater; his jaw was shadowed with stubble, his hair was wet from, she supposed, a shower, and he looked so beautiful he made her heartbeat stumble.

"Oh," she said foolishly. "That's—that's nice."

"Scrambled eggs and toast. Anna called a little while ago. She can't get in. The storm—"

"Of course." Why was he looking at her that way? Why wasn't he smiling? She was a mess, she knew, her hair all tangled, no makeup, wearing this silly robe... "Great. Just—just let me take five minutes for a shower, okay?"

"Five minutes," he said—and then he muttered something, bounded up the stairs and caught her in his arms and kissed her until she melted against him. "Five minutes," he repeated gruffly, and by the time her pulse returned to normal he was down the steps and out of sight.

Cat showered quickly, left her hair loose to air dry, pulled on jeans and a cashmere sweater and went down to the kitchen. Jake was just scooping mounds of scrambled eggs onto two plates. A platter of bacon, two mugs of coffee, napkins, silverware and a small wicker basket of toast were already on the counter.

But something was in the kitchen with them. Something dark and unpleasant. It had shown itself in those first seconds a little while ago, when Jake had looked at her, his face set and unsmiling.

Cat's nerves hummed in anticipation as she climbed onto a stool, opened a napkin and spread it in her lap.

"Mmm," she said brightly, "this looks wonderful."

"Dig in before it gets cold."

The eggs really were good. At school, scrambled eggs had been hard lumps. These were fluffy and light—and lodged in her throat just the same.

"Where'd you learn to make eggs like this?" she said, in the same artificial voice.

"I put in some time working in a restaurant when I was a kid."

"You? Working in a restaurant?"

Her surprise was genuine. Despite his mood, despite what he had to tell her, he couldn't keep from smiling.

"I worked at a lot of things growing up."

"Did your family believe work would be good for you?"

Jake laughed. "My family consisted of one person. My mother. She worked her tail off to support us. When I was old enough, or maybe I should say when I finally figured out that it was time to get my act together, I worked to help put food on the table." His tone gentled. "Don't look at me that way, Cat. We're not all born rich."

"Of course not. I just thought…" She expelled a long breath. "I don't know what I thought," she said truthfully "Except…except that something's very wrong and I want you to tell me what it is."

"Finish your supper first."

"No." Her fork clattered against her plate. "Jake. If you regret what—what we did—"

She cried out as his hands bit into her shoulders. "Regret it? Sweetheart, how could I regret something so wonderful?"

"Then what is it? You look so—so unhappy."

"Yeah." His hands dropped away from her and he got to his feet, picked up their plates and took them to the sink. "Lucas called."

It took her a moment even to remember who Lucas was.

"He wanted to apologize to you. To me, too. He said— well, he said a lot of things. Mostly he said he regrets leaving you with the wrong impression. He was—he was very taken with you, Cat."

What was this? Jake speaking on behalf of another man? Jake, who'd held her in his arms for hours and hours, telling her that someone else was taken with her?

Making love with Jake had pushed her problem aside. Now it came rushing back.

Jake had made love to her, but nothing had changed. She had to find a man to marry, and he had to see to it that she did. Otherwise she'd lose her inheritance.

But she didn't care about her inheritance. To hell with it! She'd give it up gladly to stay with Jake. How could money be more important than a once-in-a-lifetime love her lonely heart had always believed existed only in fairytales?

The question was, would Jake walk away from the pledge he'd made to Javier Estes? Would he give up whatever had made him agree to find her a husband in the first place? Was he willing to lose...?

Well, she didn't know what he'd lose. He still hadn't told her.

"Jake," she said quickly. "Jake, listen—"

"Lucas wants to see you. Tonight. He has a townhouse just a few blocks away. He's having some people in. A spur-of-the-minute blizzard party, he called it. And..." Jake's voice trailed off. He came toward her slowly, his eyes locked to her face. "If you want your inheritance," he said gruffly, "it has to be this way."

He didn't say the rest. He didn't have to. It had to be this way so that he could meet his commitment to marry her off. Whatever he'd get for that, it meant more to him than she did.

It broke her heart, but how could she fault him for it? She'd almost forgotten that she was the one in love, not Jake.

"Cat? You said you've dreamed of the freedom your inheritance will bring you. You told me that you didn't want to be trapped in yet another cage." He hesitated. "That's right, isn't it?"

"Yes," she said briskly, "it is."

"Yeah." Jake cleared his throat. It had been foolish to expect her to say anything else. He'd spent a lot of time figuring out just how to phrase the question. He wanted her to make the choice between him and her freedom rationally.

The last thing he wanted to do was play on her emotions.

He had to accept that he'd awakened her to passion, not to love. She was too young for love, too inexperienced to be tied to one man. Life, the world, all the things she'd never known, stretched ahead of her.

He loved her too much to deny her any of it.

Jake took a deep breath. "I know—I know that I took what you intended to offer to the man who marries you."

"Don't! Please—"

"I'm not going to apologize for it." Damned right he wasn't. He didn't even want to think about Cat in another man's arms. "But there has to be another way. Something else you can use to get a guy like Lucas to—to cooperate."

Catarina shook her head. "I'll just have to go through with a real marriage," she said in a small voice.

"No!" Jake took a deep breath. "No," he said, more calmly. "There must be something a rich man would—a rich man would…" He paused. A slow smile angled across his mouth. "Of course! That's it."

"What's it? What idea? What could I possibly offer? I don't have—"

"But I do." He clasped her shoulders, lifted her to her toes. "I own some land, Cat. On Maui. Beachfront property in an area where there's nothing left for sale. Lucas knows about it. We talked about it, he and I—you know, small talk at some charity thing. Hawaii, how we both liked it, how he wished he owned land there…" Jake's eyes met hers. "Lucas and I can strike a deal."

Her heart twisted with pain. A piece of land. Jake would sell it to Lucas, Lucas would agree to a marriage followed by divorce, and this would be over.

"Cat? Do you understand?"

She nodded, afraid to speak for fear she would weep instead.

"You'll get your inheritance. Your fortune. You'll be free. You'll never have to be left on the wrong side of the gates again." A muscle flickered in his jaw. His hands seemed to tighten on her. "That's what you want most in the world, you said. Isn't that right?"

Their eyes met and she waited for him to say, *Forget your inheritance, sweetheart. The only thing you need is me.*

But he didn't. He didn't say anything. Finally, when all eternity seemed to have gone by, Catarina lifted her chin and forced a little smile to her lips.

"Yes," she said, "that's exactly right, Jake. I get my money. You get—you get whatever it is you get. And then we'll both be free."

CHAPTER ELEVEN

CAT was the hit of the party.

Jake wasn't surprised. She was bright, articulate, alive with vitality and incredibly beautiful—even in this crowd, where the faces of most of the women had graced magazine covers.

A dozen men were gathered around her, smiling when she smiled, laughing when she laughed—and she laughed and smiled a lot. It wasn't because she'd had too much to drink. Not tonight. Lucas had poured her only one glass of champagne and she'd done little more than sip at it.

Tonight, Cat was laughing because she was happy. Why wouldn't she be? Her freedom was on the horizon. He'd given her the chance to say that it wasn't what she wanted...but it was.

So he'd done what he had to do. Brought her here. Handed her over to Lucas. Told him he was a good guy, that Cat liked him. The rest of it—the offer he was going to make to give Lucas those acres in Hawaii— would come later, if—hell—*when* Cat said she was ready for him to make the next move.

Talk to Lucas. Explain the situation.

Tell him he was going to give him millions of dollars' worth of beachfront if he'd agree to marry Catarina but not touch her. Not touch her. Not...

Jake lifted his glass to his lips and took a long swallow. He wasn't drinking champagne. He'd switched to Scotch. Not his favorite brand, but it didn't matter. Anything that might burn away the tightness in his chest would do tonight.

He'd deliberately faded into the background as soon as they'd arrived, though he hadn't taken his eyes from Cat. He was determined to protect her, to make sure there was no repetition of what had happened with Lucas the last time.

There wouldn't be.

Lucas had changed. He was treating Catarina with the care he'd have accorded a piece of fine crystal. He hadn't left her side, no matter how many admirers she drew. He had his arm around her waist, lightly enough to seem polite, but possessive enough so that his intentions were clear.

He was staking Cat out as his own.

Jake clenched his jaw and contemplated the pale amber liquid in his glass.

It was the best thing that could happen. Lucas was wealthy. He wouldn't give a damn about Cat's inheritance. He was a good guy, even if he hadn't seemed it before. He'd been on the make then. Tonight, when he'd phoned with the party invitation, he'd made it clear that his intentions were honorable.

"Catarina is a special young woman," he'd told Jake solemnly. "The man who wins her will be most fortunate."

Meaning Lucas had thought it over and was considering being that man.

Jake swallowed some more whiskey.

Of course that might change once he knew that Cat wouldn't be his wife in the real sense of the word. That she'd marry Lucas only if he agreed to a divorce ahead of time.

That she wouldn't sleep with him.

Four acres on the Pacific would be the trade-off. Lucas, an astute businessman, would surely accept such a deal. Any man would.

Except me, thought Jake.

He wouldn't trade the right to claim Cat as his own

for acreage on the moon. She was more precious than that. She was—

Damn.

His glass was empty. He took one last look at Cat, then crossed the room to the bar, reached for the bottle of Scotch and poured.

Soon she'd belong to Lucas. Even if she never lay in his arms she'd belong to him. To another man. Not to him. Never to—

Jake took a long mouthful of whiskey, felt it burn cleanly down his throat.

It had to be like this. Cat wanted her inheritance. Her freedom. He wanted to find the two men who were his brothers. He *had* to find them. Knowing they were out there, that he could pass them on the street and not realize they shared the same blood, would be a torment he could not endure.

Enrique must have known that when he wrote his damnable will. What else had he known? Had he laughed, planning this? Had he known Jake would lose his heart to Catarina Mendes? That he'd fall in love with—in love with—

Jake's hand trembled. He put down the glass.

That kind of thinking wasn't going to get him anywhere. He had to concentrate on the things that mattered...and, damn it, where had Lucas and Cat gone? A couple of minutes ago they'd been standing on the other side of the room. Now they'd vanished.

Jake walked through the arched doorway into the dining room. People were clustered around the table, helping themselves to the lavish buffet, but not Cat and Lucas.

The kitchen, then.

No. They weren't there, either.

His pace quickened. The door to Lucas's study was

closed. He started to knock but he got a funny feeling, flung the door open...

And found them.

Cat and Lucas. Cat, standing in the loose circle of Lucas's arms, her face turned up to his. Cat, swinging around to stare at him as the door banged against the wall, her cheeks flushed, her eyes dark with an emotion that could only be guilt.

Lucas, the son of a bitch, didn't look guilty at all. He looked like a man who'd just hit the jackpot.

"Jake," Cat said. "Jake—"

He had eyes only for Lucas. "Get your hands off her," he growled.

"Jake," Lucas said solemnly, "my friend—"

Jake grabbed Cat's wrist, swung her away from Lucas.

"Don't give me that 'friend' crap. I trusted you, you bastard. You said you understood Catarina was—"

"It's you who doesn't understand, Jake." Lucas cleared his throat. "I have asked Catarina to be my wife."

Jake blinked. How could things have moved so fast? "What?"

"She explained it all to me. I know that she must marry to gain her inheritance."

Jake looked at Cat. "You told him everything? You didn't wait to talk to me?"

"Why would I wait?" Her voice was a little shaky but her tone was defiant. "What is there to talk about?"

She was right. But so what? What did being right have to do with the growing knot of rage in Jake's gut?

"And?" he said, trying to sound calm. "He agreed to the terms?"

Cat caught her bottom lip between her teeth. "Yes, but not—not quite the way you'd planned."

Jake turned toward Lucas. "She needs to marry a

Brazilian,'' he said, as if perhaps Catarina hadn't actually gone into the details.

''Yes. I understand that.''

''A man of good character.''

Lucas stood a little taller. ''I am an attorney, a member of the trade delegation to the Embassy, and I am from an old and respected family.''

''Did she tell you the rest? That the man who marries her must agree to a marriage in name only?''

Lucas's mouth twisted. ''So Catarina said.''

''And to an immediate divorce?''

''Yes.''

The anger inside Jake began to ease. ''And you've agreed to all that?''

''For a consideration.''

''Okay. Fine.'' He forced a smile. ''I knew you'd want that property in—''

''What I want,'' Lucas said quickly, ''is the right to try and convince Catarina that our marriage should not be a temporary union.''

Jake narrowed his eyes. ''The lady's not interested.''

''I've told her that I care for her, that I am sure she will learn to care for me, and that I want her to be my wife in fact, not only in name.''

''Maybe you have a hearing problem, Estero. I just told you, the lady isn't—''

Lucas took Cat's hand. ''Why not let her speak for herself?''

''I'm speaking for her,'' Jake said coldly. ''She's my ward.''

''She's not your ward, Jake. Not in the true sense of the word.''

Jake took a step forward. ''Don't start tossing legal crap at me. Catarina is my responsibility. I make decisions for her, not you.''

"Jake." Cat's voice was low. "Jake, listen to me—"

"Be quiet," Jake said sharply.

"Watch how you speak to my fiancée, Ramirez."

"She's not your anything until I say she is."

"Jake." Catarina put her hand on his arm. "Please. We discussed this, remember? You and I agreed—"

"Let's just assume I give my permission for this marriage," Jake said, shaking off Cat's hand. "Exactly how do you propose to convince her to make it real? Are you going to sit her down, talk her to death?"

"Catarina has agreed to remain married to me for six months."

"The hell she will!"

"At the end of that time, if she still insists on divorce—"

"You want to sleep with her," Jake said bluntly.

"If you mean, I want to make love to my wife," Lucas said coldly, "you're right."

"She'll never go along with it." Jake leveled his gaze on Catarina. "Tell him," he said. "Go on, damn it. Tell him you won't sleep with him."

"We were fools to think an honorable man would agree to marry and divorce me in a heartbeat, Jake."

"You call Estero honorable? What kind of a son of a bitch would demand you climb into his bed?"

Lucas dropped Cat's hand. "Be careful what you say, Ramirez."

"It isn't like that," Cat said quickly. "He won't ask me to do anything I don't want to do."

"He's a liar," Jake growled. "He wants to take you to bed. All the rest is window-dressing."

Lucas stepped in front of Catarina. "You will not speak to Catarina that way."

"I'll speak to her any way I like."

"Keep this up," Lucas said softly, "and I'm going to ask you to step outside."

Catarina knew she would never forget Jake's smile as long as she lived.

"Why step outside?" he said, and swung a hard right that sent Lucas crumpling to the floor.

Cat didn't want to leave.

Not with him.

What she wanted was to sit on the floor beside Lucas and cradle his head in her lap even after he'd opened his eyes.

Jake wasn't having any of it.

Estero would live. His jaw would be black and blue and maybe a little swollen; his pride was definitely wounded, but he'd be fine. Jake hung around just long enough to be sure. Then he apologized to Lucas—not for punching him, but for taking a swing without warning him first.

Lucas rubbed his jaw, looked at Cat, gave Jake a strange, tight smile and said he understood.

"Well, I don't," Cat said furiously. "He hits you for no good reason, you're lying in a heap, and you tell him you understand?"

Jake muttered something and told her to stand up and get moving. When she didn't, he grabbed her hand, tugged her to her feet and propelled her out of the library, past stunned faces, onto the street and into a cab.

She wouldn't look at him, wouldn't talk to him, but that was okay. He didn't have anything he wanted to say to her, either. Actually, he was so hot with rage he figured it was better if he kept quiet.

What kind of woman was she, that she'd go from his bed to Estero's? How could he have thought he loved her? That he *had* thought it, if only for a little while, proved how screwed up this whole crazy thing had become.

Well, he knew how to solve that problem.

Let her marry Lucas. What did it matter to him? She

wanted Lucas, she could have him. The minute they were home he'd tell her that.

Except he didn't get the chance. They got into his apartment, she rounded on him like a tigress.

"How could you have done this, Jake Ramirez? Damn it, how *could* you?"

Jake stalked past her, stripping off his coat and jacket, tossing them wherever they fell, and switched on the light in the kitchen. What he wanted was another stiff belt of whiskey, but that seemed unwise. He decided to settle for a mug of the morning's coffee, reheated in the microwave.

"You ruined everything," Cat said as she stormed after him. "Nobody will marry me now. Lucas will tell every last Brazilian in the city what you did and that'll be that."

"Stop worrying," Jake said coldly. The nuker pinged; he took out the mug of coffee and took a long, bitter swallow. "I'll call Estero in the morning, tell him I made a mistake—that he can have you under whatever terms you like."

"You couldn't listen, could you? Couldn't wait long enough to let me talk!"

"Did you hear what I just said? I'll phone Estero in—"

Cat flung her purse at him. It hit the mug and hot coffee spilled over his hand. Jake hissed and dumped the mug on the counter.

"Did I burn you? Good. I'm delighted."

That was what she said, even as she grabbed Jake's hand and glared at it. It didn't look burned, but if it were, so what? Boiling in oil was what he deserved. Still, she wasn't heartless. Only Jake could lay claim to that, she thought grimly, and tugged him toward the refrigerator.

"What are you doing?"

"What does it look like I'm doing?" she snapped, depressing the lever on the ice-dispenser in the door. "I'm getting ice for your hand. Not that you deserve it. I just don't want inflicting an injury on you on my conscience."

"I don't need ice, and you didn't injure me."

Cubes dropped into her hand. She dumped them into Jake's palm and closed his fingers around them.

"No?"

"No. My hand hurt already, from… It hurt, that's all."

"It hurt because you had to play *macho* maniac and hit poor Lucas in the jaw."

"Poor Lucas will survive—and that's enough ice. You want to freeze my fingers off?"

"I want to kill you," Cat said succinctly. She let go of his hand, slapped her hands on her hips and faced him. "If only you'd listened, Ramirez, you'd have known that you had things wrong."

"The only thing I had wrong was letting myself think I was in l—"

He stopped, horrified at what he'd almost said—at the terrible truth of what he'd almost said. Because even now, damn it all, even now he still loved her.

"When you let yourself think you were in what?" Cat said, staring at him.

Jake turned away. "I let myself think I was—I was in a position to help you. Well, I can't. Not the way I intended, anyway. But that's okay. You helped yourself tonight. I told you, I'll call Estero, tell him he can do what he wants— Hey!"

Cat landed a fist like a hammer-blow between his shoulders. Jake swung toward her.

"Don't push your luck," he said. "The mood I'm in—"

"The mood *you're* in? You fool! Do you ever think that the great Joaquim Ramirez can be wrong?"

"Don't call me that."

"Why not? It's your name, isn't it?"

"My name is—"

"I know your name," she huffed. "The question is, what do *you* know? For instance, do you know that maybe, just maybe, you misinterpreted what you saw and what Lucas said?''

''Oh, right. It was such an easy scene to misinterpret,'' Jake snarled, lowering his head until they were eye to eye. ''You in Lucas's arms. Him drooling at the thought of you agreeing to sleep with—'' She swung at him again. Jake grabbed her arm and jerked it behind her back. ''Hit me again,'' he warned, ''and you'll regret it.''

Tears of anguish and of fury—at Jake for misjudging her, but mostly at herself for the foolishness of her own stupid heart—rose in Cat's eyes.

''What I regret,'' she said, ''is falling in love with you!''

''Yeah?''

''Yeah!''

''Well, let me tell you something, *senhorita*, I—'' Jake blinked. ''What did you say?''

''I said,'' Cat replied, twisting against his hand, ''you were dead wrong about Lucas.''

''That's not what you said.''

''Never mind what I said!'' Cat blew a curl off her forehead. ''We're talking about Lucas, and how you managed to jump to conclusions the size of Sugar Loaf Mountain!''

''I know what I saw. I know what Lucas said. I know what you agreed to do.''

''You don't know a thing,'' Cat huffed. ''Damnit, Jake! Let go of me!''

''Not until you tell me why I shouldn't trust my ears and eyes.''

''I would, but you're probably too thick-skulled to believe me.''

''Try me.''

''Lucas asked me why I was husband-hunting, to use your charming phrase. I told him about my inheritance, and that I had to find a suitable Brazilian husband and marry to gain it.''

"And?"

"And he said he'd been thinking things over, that perhaps t was time he found a wife. He said he'd be honored if I'd agree to be that woman. So I told him the rest. How I wanted to marry and then file for divorce. How I—I didn't want the intimacy of marriage."

"I'll bet he just loved that."

"I said," Catarina continued, her eyes narrowing, "that you would give him that land in Maui if he agreed to my terms."

"And?"

"And, he said he didn't want the land, he wanted me."

"At least he's not a complete fool," Jake snapped. "So, what next? You just said, 'Okay, fine. I'll sleep with you'?"

He could feel the tremor of anger that rippled through her. "You're a horrible man. Has anyone ever told you that?"

"Only you, baby."

"Perhaps it's because I'm the only one who knows the real Joaquim Ramirez."

"I said—"

"Don't call you that. I know. I just don't understand the reason."

Jake's jaw tightened. "I'll tell you the reason. It's because the name reminds me of who I really am. A rich man's bastard."

Cat's eyes widened. "Oh, Jake—"

"That's why I had to agree to find you a husband." His hand fell away from her. "All my life I thought the man who sired me died a hero, died before he could come back and marry my mother. A few weeks ago I found out the truth. He abandoned her. Left her to have me, raise me, alone."

"Jake—"

"I also learned that he spawned two other bastards," he

said bitterly. "Do you understand, Cat? I have brothers ou
there somewhere, but the only way my father's lawyer wil
give me their names is if I complete this—this travesty o
a guardianship and find a husband for you." His hand
closed on her shoulders and he hauled her to her toes. "How
could I have known I'd fall in love with you? How in hel
could I possibly have known that?"

She stared at him. "What?"

"I said I love you, damn it! I love you more than I eve
dreamed a man could love a woman—and what good has i
done? You slept with me. Now you've agreed to sleep with
Lucas—"

Cat's hand whipped through the air. She hit Jake hard
enough to make his head snap back.

"I hate you," she sobbed. "Hate you, hate you…"

Jake caught her in his arms and crushed her mouth be
neath his. When she struggled, he clasped her face, tunneled
his fingers into her hair and held her captive to his kiss.

"Hate you," she sighed, when he lifted his mouth jus
long enough to change the angle of the kiss, and then she
wrapped her arms around his neck and kissed him back.

A long time later, he leaned his forehead against hers.

"Say the words, sweetheart," he whispered.

"I love you," Cat said softly. "I love you with all my
heart."

Jake shuddered with relief. Then he drew her close, held
her tightly against him and knew that he would never, ever
let her go.

"All I agreed to do with Lucas was live under his roof
for six months," Cat said. "He was sure I'd change my
mind about the divorce once I got to know him." She drew
back a little, enough so she could see Jake's face. "I told
him he was wrong and he said he'd take his chances. Tha
was his demand, Jake. Mine was that we'd live together as

friends. There would be no sex. Lucas said he'd abide by that. He gave his word of honor.''

His word of honor. Jake knew that Lucas would be bound by it.

He'd been wrong. About Cat. About Lucas. About everything but what really mattered.

His love for Catarina.

Jake cleared his throat. "Cat?" He tilted her face to his. "In all this time you've never asked me how much money you're going to inherit." He paused. "It's twenty-five million dollars, sweetheart.''

Her eyes widened. "So much? I never dreamed—''

"That'll buy a lot of independence." He hesitated. All this had only just come to him. Would she agree to it? For the first time in his adult life Jake Ramirez was scared. "Cat. I love you.''

Her eyes glittered with tears. "And I love you.''

"I want you to be my wife.''

There were no more beautiful words in the world than those—but they broke Catarina's heart.

"Oh, Jake, I can't. I can't! If I do—''

"If you do, you'll lose that money." His mouth was dry. "I understand. But you won't lose your independence, honey. I'll see to that. I'll support you as a good husband should—and I'll make you a gift of the same amount your parents left you. You can put it into a bank account under your own name. I'll have no access to it, no rights, no... What?''

"Jake, my love." Tears streamed down Cat's cheeks. "I'd give up the money in a heartbeat. Don't you know that? I'd give up the world to spend the rest of my life with you... But I can't.''

"What do you mean, you can't? You just said—''

"If I don't marry according to the dictates of my parents' will, you won't be able to fulfill the conditions of your father's will! You'll never know the names of your brothers. And—and I love you too much to do that to you."

She started to turn away. Jake wouldn't let her. He clasped her hands, brought them to his chest so she could feel the beat of his heart.

"Listen to me, Catarina."

"There's nothing you can say that will—"

"I lived thirty years without knowing these men existed. I'll regret not finding out who they are, sure." His hands tightened on hers. "But I can't imagine what my life would be like without you."

How could she lie to him when his eyes were locked to hers?

"It would be empty," she whispered, "as mine will be without you."

"Cat, I love you. I adore you. If you think I'm going to let you walk away, you're wrong."

"I can't do this to you, Jake. I told you, I love you too much to—"

He kissed her. Slowly. Tenderly. When finally he lifted his head her mouth was trembling.

"I love you," he said again. "Besides," he added softly, "the key to this mess isn't in your hands. It's in mine."

"What do you mean? If I marry the right man—"

"Yeah, but you won't. If you won't marry me, I won't let you marry anyone else. You need my approval for the guy you pick, remember?"

Did she? Or could she marry anyone as long as he met the standards of the will? Jake didn't remember and didn't care. What he'd just said sounded good and he wasn't about to back away from it.

"You understand, Cat?" he said sternly. "It's me or nobody. You want us to end up two stubborn people, going through life alone? It's up to you."

Her future, his, a lifetime of love and joy stretched ahead.

They were the richest gifts a man could give a woman, and Jake was offering them to her.

"Are you sure?"

Jake drew her against him and kissed her again. This time when he lifted his head her eyes were soft.

"Oh, Jake. I love you so much."

"Enough to marry me?"

"Yes. Yes. Yes..."

Jake gathered her close, kissed her until the world was spinning beneath their feet.

"I'm not going to give you the chance to change your mind," he whispered, rocking her in his arms.

She looked up so he could see her smile. "I have no intention of changing my mind, *senhor*. You forget how stubborn I can be."

"In that case I won't insist on our wedding taking place tomorrow." Jake laughed at the expression on her face. "Next week will be fine. That'll give me time to introduce you to my mother, and for Belle to take you shopping for a wedding gown."

"Your mother might want to come, too."

"Yeah," he said gruffly. "Come to think of it, she might. You'll like her, sweetheart. She's a strong woman, the same as you." He kissed the tip of her nose. "You have any special place in mind for the ceremony?"

"Yes. Right here, Jake. In your home."

"In *our* home."

She smiled. "If we're lucky, it might snow."

"Perfect."

Cat lifted her mouth to his. "I adore you, Joaquim."

Somehow, the name sounded right on her lips.

"You'd better," he said gruffly. "I don't know what I'd do if you didn't."

They stayed locked in each other's arms for long moments. Then Jake drew back.

"I should call Estes."

"What...? Oh. The lawyer." Cat's smile dimmed. "Jake? Are you sure? You can still change—"

"I'm sure," he said firmly. "I'll never change my mind, honey. I promise you that."

It was almost as if Estes had been waiting for the call, because he answered on the first ring.

"*Senhor* Estes," Jake said quietly, "this is Jake Ramirez. Yes. I'm fine, thank you. Yes, *Senhorita* Mendes is also fine." He drew Cat closer. "*Senhor,,* we have some news for you. I've found a husband for the *senhorita*. Yes, she's happy about it. Of course—if you like." He held the phone to Cat's ear. "He wants to talk to you."

"Hello, *Senhor* Estes. *Sim, eu sou muito bem, obrigado. Sim, eu sou muito feliz.*" She listened, then smiled up at Jake. "He wants you again."

Jake put the phone to his ear. "*Senhor* Estes. I have more news, but you won't be pleased to hear it. You see, the husband I've found for Catarina is me." His eyes met Cat's. "I love her," he said simply, "and she loves me. We understand the ramifications, that she's forfeiting her inheritance and I'm forfeiting the right to know who my half-brothers are, but—"

Cat, watching her lover's face, was baffled by what she saw. Jake's brows shot toward the ceiling, his mouth dropped open, then curved until his grin stretched from ear to ear.

"What?" she whispered.

He started to laugh.

"What?" she said, but louder.

"Yes," Jake said. "Yes, of course. I can't believe I didn't...Yes. *Sim, Senhor* Estes. *Sim.* Goodbye for now. And thank you. Thank you very much."

"*Sim?*" Cat repeated, starting at him. "Since when do you speak Portuguese? And what's so fun—?"

Her words became a squeal as Jake swung her up into his arms and spun in a circle.

"Jake? What's going on?"

"A miracle," he said, and kissed her.

"What miracle? For goodness' sakes, tell me what's happening!"

"*Senhorita* Mendes." Jake laughed out loud. "It turns out you're going to marry a suitable Brazilian husband after all."

Cat stiffened in his arms. "No! Jake, you said—"

"Me, sweetheart. I'm that guy."

"You?"

"My old man was a Brazilian citizen. His name and nationality are right there on my birth certificate. That gives me dual citizenship. I'm American…and I'm Brazilian." He tried, and failed, to look stern and serious. "And, as you well know, I'm a very proper man."

It took a moment to sink in. When it did, Cat began to smile.

"That means our marriage will fulfill the terms of my parents' will and of Enrique's, too."

"You'll get your inheritance."

"I don't care about that! What matters is that Estes will tell you the names of your brothers."

"Better than that. The three of us are going to meet in his office."

"When?"

"He'll phone with the date."

Cat's smile broadened. "That wily old fox. He knew, didn't he? He *knew* we were meant for each other…and so did your father."

My father, Jake thought, trying the words for size. Was it possible? At this point he was willing to admit it might be.

"Maybe. But right now…" Jake's arms tightened around

Catarina. "Right now I think you should know something about proper Brazilian husbands."

She caught his teasing tone. Smiling, she linked her hands behind his neck.

"What's that, *senhor?*"

"They believe that snowy nights and snowy days should be spent in bed."

Jake began to climb the stairs with Cat in his arms. She pressed her lips to his throat.

"What about starry nights and sunny days?"

"Bed," he said solemnly.

"And rainy nights?"

"And rainy days." Jake shouldered open the door to his bedroom. *To our bedroom,* he thought, and his heart filled with joy.

"In fact," he said softly, "I can't think of a better place to spend the rest of our lives, sweetheart."

"Neither can I," Cat whispered, and drew his mouth down to hers for a kiss.

CHAPTER TWELVE

MAYBE there came a time in every man's life when he felt unnecessary.

Superfluous might be more accurate.

Jake introduced his mother to his bride-to-be at Sarah's apartment on Sutton Place, had all of an evening to beam as he watched the women in his life form an instant bond...and then discovered what all men discover when the word "wedding" is spoken.

He was unnecessary, superfluous and, more to the point, in the way.

"A wedding next week?" his mother said in horror. "It isn't possible! Catarina? Tell my son we need more time than that to get ready."

"More time for what?" said Jake, in his innocence.

"For what, he asks." Sarah rolled her eyes at Catarina, who smiled at Jake but rolled her eyes right back at her mother-in-law-to-be.

"Where will you have the ceremony? The reception?"

"At my place. *Our* place," Jake said, taking Cat's hand.

Cat nodded and wove her fingers through his. "The ceremony before that wonderful fireplace in the living room, and with the doors to the library flung open for the reception."

"Perfect."

That was it, then, Jake thought—but his women had launched into female-speak. It didn't take him long to realize he'd never understand the language.

"Who'll do the flowers?"

Who'll do the flowers? What was there to do? You

phoned the florist, ordered a corsage. Two corsages. Okay, two corsages and a boutonnière. Okay, yeah, and maybe a bouquet for the mantel.

"And the caterer. Of course it depends on the time of day. Brunch is always nice."

Brunch? Brunch was definitely a word in female-speak. No man Jake had ever met could make sense of a meal that was neither breakfast or lunch.

"And musicians," Sarah said. "Three pieces, perhaps. A pianist, a violinist, a cellist. And of course you'll have to find the right gown."

"Honey?" Jake cleared his throat. "I thought we were going to have a small wedding."

"We will," his mother said, answering for Catarina, "but that doesn't mean it can't be beautiful. Isn't that right, Catarina?"

Jake looked at Cat. Her eyes were shining; she had the same little smile on her lips as the one on that Italian lady in the portrait that hung in the Louvre.

"Well," she said softly, "flowers and some music would be nice. What do you think, Jake?"

What Jake thought, as he gazed at the woman he loved, was that he was an idiot. His Cat had spent years in the austere surroundings of a convent school. If she wanted a wedding with all the trimmings, by God, she'd have one.

Smiling, he put an arm around each of his women.

"I think all of it would be nice," he said bravely. "The gown, the musicians, the caterer, the flowers. Everything you want, sweetheart."

Cat touched her hand to his face. "I already have everything I want," she said softly. "I have you."

Sarah Reece, who had watched her son go from troubled boy to determined man, who'd watched him earn the millions that had changed her life and his, knew that what she was seeing now was all that mattered.

Her Joaquim was happy.

She held back until the lovers had kissed her goodbye
and left. Then she let the tears come. After a while, she
sighed, put on her coat and went to a little church nearby.
There, in its comforting silence, she lifted her face to the
vaulted darkness and sent a message to a man she hated for
abandoning her and loved for giving her Jake.

"Enrique," she said softly, "wherever you are...thank
you for finally doing something right."

They were married a month later, before the fireplace that
was garlanded with white and pink roses.

Sarah had arranged everything, with Belle's help. A handful of Jake's friends—friends who now were Cat's—at-
tended the ceremony and the brunch that followed.

The bride was beautiful, the groom handsome. Most people thought they were crazy to head north to the Adirondack
Mountains for their honeymoon. The winter, everyone
pointed out, was an especially snowy one; didn't they want
to go where it was warm and sunny?

"We like snow," Jake said, and Cat blushed and buried
her face in his shoulder.

The day after they returned home a letter was hand-
delivered to Jake's office. The vellum envelope, bearing a
Brazilian stamp, was marked "Private" and "*Confidencial.*"

Jake felt a tightness in his throat when he saw it—he had
not heard from Javier Estes since he'd phoned him with
news of his marriage to Catarina—but he waited until he
got home that night to open it.

He wanted his wife with him.

They sat before the fireplace in their bedroom. Jake took
a deep breath and tore open the envelope.

He wasn't sure what he'd expected to see below the now-
familiar name of Javier Estes. The attorney had promised
Jake a meeting with his brothers, but perhaps he'd changed

his mind. Perhaps he'd simply sent two names, two addresses and telephone numbers.

What he found was a note written in Estes's hand. Jake read aloud. "'*Dear Mr. Ramirez, I am sure you will be happy to learn that your half-brothers have also successfully completed their tasks.*'" He looked up at Cat. "I figured they'd have to jump through some hoops, too." He took her hand and kissed it. "Thank God my jump led to you."

She smiled and squeezed his hand. "Go on," she said. "Read the rest."

"'*If you wish to meet them, please appear at my office promptly at four in the afternoon on the fourteenth of February.*' If I wish to meet them," Jake said, and made a choked sound that was supposed to be a laugh.

Cat kissed him. "Only another few weeks! Oh, Jake, how wonderful."

"There's more."

He read the final paragraph.

"'*You will, at the same time, receive a check representing your share in your late father's estate.*'"

Estes had thoughtfully translated the amount of the inheritance into American dollars. Jake read it aloud.

It was an amazing figure.

"He probably stole it from widows and orphans," Jake growled, though he knew that wasn't true. One of the things he'd learned about his father was that Enrique had inherited a fortune and more than tripled it during his lifetime. "I already told Estes what he could do with that money. I sure as hell won't touch it."

Cat put her hand on his. "Maybe your brothers can put your share to good use."

"If they're anything like me," Jake said decisively, "they won't want it, either."

But that was the question, wasn't it? he thought later that night, as he lay in bed with his wife asleep in his arms.

Were his half-brothers like him? Or were they like the man who'd sired them?

Another couple of months and he'd know.

They flew to Rio a few days before the scheduled meeting.

Jake had rented a duplex at Ipanema. The terrace, which overlooked the gorgeous beach, had its own private pool. After a little coaxing he convinced Catarina that the only way to enjoy that privacy was to swim nude—and to make love under the hot Brazilian sun.

"Wicked man," Cat whispered the first time, in such a throaty purr as her body arched to his that Jake grinned and said yeah, and wasn't she glad he was?

They walked on the beach, watched the sunset from the rocks at Arpoadaor, discovered tiny restaurants and elegant boutiques. At Jake's urging Cat bought the kind of bikini that befitted a *carioca,* even though she refused to wear it anywhere but on their terrace—for him. They danced until dawn, swaying together to the hot, sensual beat of Rio's music.

And then, at last, it was the fourteenth of February.

Jake awoke early, immediately aware that this was the day. Whatever happened at four o'clock would surely change his life.

He dropped a light kiss on his sleeping wife's mouth, slipped on a pair of shorts and went out on the terrace.

Moments later Cat came up behind him, slid her arms around his waist and kissed his back.

"Good morning," she said softly.

"I'm sorry I woke you, sweetheart," he said, drawing her to his side.

"I put up the coffee."

"Great."

They stood in silence, watching a lone jogger on the beach below. Then Cat sighed.

"It's going to be fine, Jake."

There was no point pretending he didn't know what she meant.

"It's going to *be*. That's all I know," he said gruffly. "I'm meeting two strangers whose genes I share, and when I do... Well, who knows? They might turn out to be guys I'd like to know better or—"

"They will," Catarina said quickly. "I feel it in my bones."

He looked down at her and smiled. "Such beautiful bones."

She smiled, too. Then she turned in his arms and faced him. "I love you, Joaquim Ramirez."

Jake tilted her face to his. "And that's all that matters," he said, and knew in his heart it was true.

And yet, he thought, and yet how incredible it would be if his brothers turned out to be men he'd be proud to call his friends.

A little after two-thirty he kissed Cat goodbye and took a taxi to the offices of Javier Estes. He'd figured on traffic. Besides, by then he'd been pacing the terrace like a trapped animal.

"Go," Cat had said gently, when he'd said maybe he ought to get started.

But when he stepped out of the cab he still had forty minutes to kill. No way was he going up to Estes's office to wait that out.

The street could have been one in New York. Tall buildings crowded together, but he could see a break in the unrelenting glass and steel forest right across the way, where a neon sign said *Café*.

Jake checked for a break in the stream of cars and trucks, found one and jogged toward it.

The café was a cool, dimly lit oasis. Leather booths,

mostly unoccupied, stretched the length of one wall, and a zinc bar stood to the right, where a lone bartender was polishing glasses. The man acknowledged Jake with a polite smile and a lift of his eyebrows.

"*Um whisky, por favor,*" Jake said.

The bartender nodded. "Sorry," he said, in perfect English. "I thought the girl served you before she went on her break."

"I'm afraid you have me confused with another patron," Jake said politely.

The bartender cocked his head. "Yeah. Now that I take a second look..." He nodded. "Whiskey, you said? Scotch?"

"Yeah. Laphroaig, if you have it, and bottled water on the—"

"Side." Another smile as the bartender poured the drink, then the water. "Amazing."

"What is?" Jake said, as he took out his wallet and put down some bills.

"That guy in the back. The last booth. He ordered Laphroaig, too, with bottled water on the side, and he looks enough like you to be your— Hey! Hey, you forgot your whiskey!"

The man in the last booth had risen to his feet and was staring at Jake. Jake returned the stare.

The hair rose on the back of his neck.

He could have been looking into a mirror.

Everything was the same. Height. Weight. Build. The ink-black hair that curled over his forehead no matter how he tried to prevent it. Green eyes. Even that little indentation in the chin he'd nicked a dozen times as a kid, first learning to shave.

Hell, the guy was his doppelganger.

Jake swallowed hard and walked toward the back of the room just as the other man began moving toward him. They met mid-way, and now Jake could see there were differences. It was the same face, the same build—and yet it wasn't. The shape of the nose, of the eyes. Half an inch or so in height. The man facing him had a little less curl in his hair at the temples...

Jake cleared his throat.

"Are you...?" he said, just as the stranger opened his mouth and said the same words. Both of them hesitated.

"My name," Jake said, "is—is Ramirez."

The other man nodded. "Yes. Same here. Ramirez. Luis Ramirez." He gave a little laugh. "Or Anton Scott-Lee. Depends on the time and place."

"Jake," Jake said. "Jake Ramirez. Or Joaquim." Somehow he dredged up an answering laugh. "Depends on the time and place—and maybe on my mood."

"I know exactly what you mean." Anton held out his hand and Jake took it. "Jake—good to meet you."

"Same here, Luis. Or is it Anton?"

"Anton's the name I grew up with."

"I grew up with Jake."

"Well, then, Anton and Jake it is."

The men went on staring at each other. Then they smiled and ended the prolonged clasping of hands.

"So," Jake said briskly, "is that a British accent?"

"I should hope so," Anton said, his smile turning into a grin. "And you're American?"

"Yes."

"Well—"

"Well—"

"I don't believe this," a gruff voice said, and a third man joined them. He was tall. Had black hair. Green eyes. A cleft in his chin. He stared from Anton to Jake. "Don't tell me," he said softly. "You're both named—"

"Ramirez," Jake said. "And so are you."

"Yes. Nicholas. Nick. I'm—I'm..."

"Australian?" Anton ventured.

Nick grinned. "Right. I'm just stunned. We look like a three-way mirror."

"Triplets," Anton said, grinning in return.

"Or a vaudeville routine," Jake offered.

The men laughed. Then Anton gestured to the booth. "Shall we? I was just having a—"

"Scotch?" Jake said, checking the pale amber color of the liquid in the glass.

"Right. I'll get the barman. You'll want…?"

"Here you are, gentlemen," the bartender said briskly, coming up beside them. "Two Laphroaigs, bottled water on the side—just the same as this first—" His eyes widened. "Hello. I guess it doesn't take a genius to figure out that you guys are brothers, huh?"

Jake, Anton and Nick looked at each other. Anton swallowed hard. "No," he said softly, "I guess it doesn't."

They had dozens of things in common, and they'd yet to touch on their individual stories. Too complicated to go into now, with the clock ticking, Nick said. Jake and Anton agreed.

But all the rest was amazing. The sports they played. The places they enjoyed. Their preferences in Scotch whiskey. Their determination to make their own way in the world.

Their ideas of what constituted a desirable woman. Physical beauty, yes. But much more than that.

A woman had to be independent.

"Fiercely," Jake said, "even when it can be a pain in the…butt."

His brothers grinned, raised their glasses and touched them together.

She had to be strong.

"Strong as only a woman can be," Anton said quietly, and they touched glasses again.

"Independent, strong…and with a generous heart," Nick added.

Another ceremonial touching of the glasses and a celebratory swallow of whiskey.

"My Cat—Catarina—is all those things," Jake said. "My bride."

It turned out all three were newly married, and crazy about their wives.

"Wait until you meet my Tess," Nick said.

"You'll be crazy about my Cristina," Anton said.

Smiles all around. Then Jake's smile faded.

"I hate him," he said quietly.

"Enrique?" Nick and Anton said, in one voice.

"Yeah. I didn't even know he existed until a few months ago."

Anton lifted his glass and looked at it as if it held deep secrets. "Neither did I."

"Well, I knew he existed," Nick said carefully. "I even met him."

His brothers stared at him. "And? What was he like?"

There was a long silence. Then Nick shrugged. "There was a time I'd have said our father was soulless."

"And now?" Anton said, leaning forward.

"And now I suspect he was a man, just like us—except he didn't realize what being a man actually meant until death was staring him in the face."

Another silence. Then Jake let out a breath.

"Maybe you're right. It's a long story, but this last thing he did—"

"Enrique?"

"Yeah. Enrique. Our father," he said, testing the words for the first time. "The last thing he did—what he set out for me in that will—is what led me to my wife. So I suppose—I suppose I owe him something for that."

His brothers nodded. "The same here," Nick said, and Anton quickly agreed.

"Still…" Jake said carefully, because even though they'd discovered so many shared convictions he didn't know how they'd feel about the money their father had left them. "Still," he said, "I don't want his money. If you guys do, that's okay, but—"

"I've already told Estes what he can do with my third," Anton said.

"Graphically, I hope," Nick added, and the three men laughed.

Jake raised a hand and signaled for another round.

"Actually, my wife will get my share," Anton said. "It's a long story, but Enrique set things up so that if I refuse the money Cristina inherits it instead." His smile broadened. "And she's going to put it to good use. She has a ranch, and there's a forest that needs protecting…" He shook his head. "Another tale that's too long to tell just now, but trust me, the money will be well-spent."

"So will my share," Nick said. "Tess suggested we donate it to an orphanage. I think that's perfect."

"Yeah," Jake said, "it's a great idea."

"And what about you?" Anton asked.

Jake frowned. "I never got much further than figuring I'd dump the money in the sea. But listening to the two of you gives me an idea. I mean, it's not the money that's tainted, it's how our father tried to use it." He paused until the bartender had served their drinks. "My Catarina had a tough childhood, shut away in a boarding school about as welcoming as a mausoleum." Smiling, he raised his glass. "Gentlemen, here's to the fund that will establish the Catarina Elena Teresa Mendes-Ramirez School for Girls—*Girls*, not Young Ladies!"

His brothers and he touched glasses again and tossed back their drinks. Then Nick looked at his watch.

"Jake. Anton. It's almost time."

Jake nodded. "Then let's do it."

"First, though," Nick said, "I want to call Tess. She was, uh, she was a little concerned about how this would go."

"Yes," Anton said, with a smile, "Cristina was, too."

"Add Cat to the list." Jake took out a cell phone. So did his brothers. "Uh, Anton? Nick?" He spoke carefully, because even though things had gone well—better than well—you never knew. "Before we call our wives…"

His brothers raised their eyebrows. "What?"

"Well, I was thinking… There's this terrific restaurant a couple of blocks from where Cat and I are staying. Nothing flashy or trendy, just the kind of place where we could get a table for six and spend the evening getting to know each other."

Neither man answered. Jake flushed.

"No problem," he said briskly. "I understand."

"You don't," Nick said, a little thickly. "I was just—I was just having—you know—a little trouble getting the words out."

"Same here." Anton's voice was husky. "I think your idea is great."

"Great," Nick echoed. "So, come on, man. Tell us the name of the restaurant."

The three men smiled. Then each dialed a number. Each turned away and spoke softly to the woman he adored—the women their father had somehow arranged for them to meet.

Moments later, the three Ramirez brothers walked out into the sunshine—together.

Together for all time.

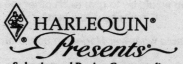

Coming Next Month

HARLEQUIN *Presents*

THE BEST HAS JUST GOTTEN BETTER!

#2505 BLACKMAILING THE SOCIETY BRIDE Penny Jordan
Jet-Set Wives

Lucy was facing huge debts after divorcing her cheating husband.
Millionaire Marcus Canning needed an heir—and a wife. Lucy knew
Marcus wanted her for convenience—but she'd always loved him, and
she couldn't resist his passionate lovemaking....

#2506 THE GREEK'S CHRISTMAS BABY Lucy Monroe
Christmas theme

Greek tycoon Aristide Kouros has a piece of paper to prove that
he's married, but no memory of his beautiful wife, Eden. Eden loves
Aristide and it's breaking her heart that he has no recollection of their
love. But Eden has a secret that will bind Aristide to her forever....

#2507 SLEEPING WITH A STRANGER Anne Mather
Foreign Affairs

Helen Shaw's holiday on the island of Santos should be relaxing. But
then she sees Greek tycoon Milos Stephanides. Years ago they had an
affair—until, discovering he was untruthful, Helen left him. Now she
has something to hide from Milos....

#2508 TAKEN BY THE HIGHEST BIDDER Jane Porter
For Love or Money

In Monte Carlo Baroness Samantha van Bergen has been wagered—
and won by darkly sexy Italian racing driver Cristiano Bartolo. Virginal
Sam is scared Cristiano will seduce her—but she quickly discovers he
has another reason for wanting her. Bedding her is just a bonus...!

#2509 HIS WEDDING-NIGHT HEIR Sara Craven
Wedlocked!

Since fleeing her marriage to Sir Nicholas Tempest, Cally Maitland has
become accustomed to life on the run. But Nicholas isn't prepared
to let Cally go. He has a harsh ultimatum: give him their long-overdue
wedding night—and provide him with an heir!

#2510 CLAIMING HIS CHRISTMAS BRIDE Carole Mortimer
Christmas theme

When Gideon Webber meets Molly Barton he wants her badly. But
he is convinced she is another man's mistress....Three years later
a chance meeting throws Molly back in his path, and this time he's
determined to claim her—as his wife.